CW00549244

CATHY SCOTT: DARK QUEEN

BEHIND THE MIRROR BOOK IV

TOBEY ALEXANDER

TAGS CREATIVE

For my daughter, Little Miss, who insisted that Cathy needed her own story. There's always room for more adventure, never forget that.

CHAPTER ONE

FAMILY TIME

Cathy Scott was beyond fed up as she sat on the Welsh beach looking out across the rolling sea. The breeze had lifted, and she watched as Aiden and Timothy attempted to scale the massive rocks that surrounded the bay.

'Be careful, you two!' Her mother hollered as Aiden, now sixteen, took a daring leap between two outcrops of rock. 'Why doesn't he ever listen, eh, Cathy?'

Rather than answer, Cathy offered a shrug and dropped her attention to Evie, who lay by her side. She was only three, but already a sizeable dog that doted on Cathy. She had arrived soon after they had all returned from Mielikuvitus and she suspected it had been her parent's way of helping ease the pain at having lost her friend in the battle.

At first Cathy had wanted to name the dog Minnie, after the minotaur that had befriended her in Mielikuvitus, but her dad had talked her out of it. Instead, she had named the dog after her great-grandmother at the suggestion of her dad.

'Fancy a walk, Eevs?' Cathy ruffled the dog's ears as she watched Timothy try in vain to follow his older brother's path.

Rising from the towel, Cathy looked at her mother, who was once again sat back with her nose buried in a book.

'Can I go explore?' Cathy quizzed as she dusted the sand from her legs. 'I'll take Evie with me. I won't go far.'

'Can't you sit and just enjoy the beach?' Her mother answered as she turned the page. 'I've already got the boys acting like they're climbing Everest!'

'I'm more sensible than them!' Cathy huffed.

'I know you are.' Her dad interrupted as he shielded his eyes from the sun. 'It won't do any harm Susan. Cathy's sensible enough not to wander too far.'

'Fine,' her mother groaned. 'No further than the house on the cliffs.'

'But,'

'Listen to your mother!'

'Ok.'

Looking across the wide stretch of beach in the bay they had found, Cathy realised there was nobody else around. Everyone else had preferred the main beach that lay on the far side of the rocks, whereas this particular stretch of pale sand was a little more off the beaten track. Casting a glance at her brothers, she scooped up Evie's lead and slipped it over her head.

'You'll probably want to put her on the lead,' her dad added as she prepared to go exploring.

'She'll be fine.'

'Just keep in mind other people might worry about how big she is.'

As Evie rose and shook off the sand from her white coat, Cathy realised how intimidating her best-friend would seem. Coming up to her chest, the white

Siberian Laika was a formidable animal. As Cathy ruffled her face, she saw the almost wolfish appearance of Evie's face and smiled to herself.

'You'll be a good girl with me, won't you?'

Almost skipping across the sand, Cathy left her parents behind and moved towards the shoreline, where the crystal water lapped against the sand. Stepping into the sea, Cathy shuddered at the chilly water but soon scrambled her way up onto a seaweed covered rock jutting from the surface of the sea.

She loved it here. Somehow it reminded her of Mielikuvitus and the time she had spent there what felt like an age ago. Even though she had only been eight at the time, the memories still replayed in her dreams, and she longed to return to the magical land behind the mirrors in the cellar. Since coming back though, her parents had been adamant than none of them should return unless Sky, or the Elders, called for them.

Sometimes Cathy feared it had all been a dream. While Aiden had grown up and had his attentions on other things besides magical lands and fantastical creatures, Timothy still had his connection with Mielikuvitus. In a way, it had brought Cathy and her brother closer together, but even he was getting older.

Timothy still had the advantage of his Ecilop, Aleobe, who had been allowed to stay with him while Cathy had left that world with nothing. She had often wondered why Sky had not given her an Ecilop of her own, but when she had tried to ask her parents about it, they had avoided the subject.

'I've got you instead, though.' Cathy muttered to Evie, who walked by her side across the rocks.

Hearing the chatter of seagulls above her, Cathy paused and watched a half dozen birds scatter from the rocks in front of her. As they launched into the cloudless sky, she noted the house perched on the jagged cliffs at the far side of the secluded bay.

The house looked haunted. That was the first thing Cathy had thought when she had seen it silhouetted against the bright sea. Having walked past it every morning since they had arrived, Cathy had never seen anyone at the house, but now there was a curious old woman pottering around on the grass by the side of the enormous house.

Watching the old woman, Cathy made her way towards the house and the uneven cliffs that somehow held it in place and stopped the house from tumbling into the ocean. As she inched closer towards the impressive house, Cathy tried her best to count off the chimney pots silhouetted against the bright sky.

As an enormous wave crashed against the rocks ahead of her, Cathy was forced to shield her face as a spray of seawater carried in the wind and soaked her from head to foot. As Evie bolted to an outcrop of jagged stone to avoid the spray, Cathy couldn't help but laugh as she wiped her sodden hair from her face.

'You've had the better idea, Eevs!' Cathy chortled as she adjusted her blonde hair and tied it into a ponytail with the hair band she had kept around her wrist. 'Want to go back?'

As if answering her, Cathy smiled as Evie leapt up onto the nearest stone and continued along the path around the bay towards the far side of the house. As Cathy passed beneath the outcrop of rock that somehow remained in position with the lawn above and nothing but air between the sea and the rough stone, she realised how spooky and mysterious the old house looked.

Even from the distance of the sand, the house had an ominous air about it. Now, standing in its shadow, there was something odd about the house. So many windows looked out in every direction, but Cathy could see nothing about the house inside. The stonework was pitted with debris from years of exposure to the sea, but there was one particular element that unnerved Cathy as she moved around the side of the house.

High above, etched into the brickwork that made up one chimney glaring down at her, was a weathered face. Shielding her eyes to look up, Cathy reckoned it had once been a person's face carved into the stone. But now the surface was rough and weathered. The only feature that remained were the hollow eyes. The whipping sea winds had carved the face and stolen its features to look almost like smoke wrapped in the shape of a head.

As Cathy was about to take another step, her foot caught on a jagged edge of rock and she felt her legs go from underneath her. At the same time, another wave crashed into the face of the rocks and as she landed painfully on the rough stone, she was once again soaked from head to toe.

'Ouch!' Was all she could yelp as her forehead crashed into the stone where Evie had been standing and immediately she saw stars.

Holding back the tears, Cathy wiped the stinging seawater from her eyes and looked up at the bright blue sky above her. Not wanting to move, she felt the warmth of blood trickling down her forehead. Pressing her fingers above her right eye, Cathy smeared the blood that oozed from a snaking cut above her eyebrow.

In an instant Evie was on her. Having been unable to avoid the wave, Evie's coat was soaked through and a piece of seaweed had wrapped itself around her tail. As she bounded over to Cathy's side, there was somehow a look of concern on the dog's face.

'I'm fine,' Cathy groaned, as she sat up. 'I'm fine Eevs.'

Feeling a wave of dizziness wash over her, Cathy chanced a look back to the beach and felt surprise to see how far around the rocks she had gone. There was no sign of her parents, or her brothers, from where she sat, and she felt very much alone. Looking back the way she had come, the crashing waves had brought with it a carpet of slippery seaweed that now clung to every inch of the stones and rocks.

'I don't think we'll be going back that way.' Cathy muttered to herself as she hoisted herself up to her feet. 'Lets get back to mum and dad. I think I might need a plaster on this.'

Feeling Evie's gaze on her, Cathy wiped the blood from her head with the back of her hand and continued along the path they had started on. No longer paying attention to the enormous house above them, Cathy moved as fast as she dared until she found herself facing a dead end.

Reaching the furthest side of the rocks, Cathy found their way blocked by the sea and a sheer drop onto the next level of rocks. Feeling her heart sink, she turned to look at Evie. As her eyes dropped to her damp companion, she caught sight of something odd about the rocks beneath the overhanging lawn.

Moving closer, she soon realised that a set of crude steps had been carved into the stone. Following them with her eyes, Cathy felt a wave of relief as the steps led up towards the eerie house on the cliffs. As another wave threatened to wash her and Evie over the edge of the stone, Cathy made her choice and called Evie to her side as she shuffled herself up the narrow steps towards the overhanging lawn.

CHAPTER TWO

HOUSE ON THE ROCKS

With great care, Cathy followed the carved steps as they wound around the rock face. There was no edge or railing to her left side as she followed them over the expanse of sea she had been looking at moments before. Awash with nervousness, Cathy brushed her shoulder against the stone, as if it would keep her from falling.

After what felt like an age creeping up the steps, she felt a wave of relief as her head lifted above the level of the lawn. Wasting no time moving away from the unsafe edge, Cathy scrambled onto the grass and looked up at the house.

The impressive mansion covered the sun and Cathy felt a chill in the sudden shadow from where the sea had soaked her. Taking a moment to compose herself, she took in the impressive home that now looked easily three times as big as she had imagined. Once again her eyes fell to the weathered face high above, near the eaves of the pitched roof, and she shuddered at the distorted and weathered face.

'Excuse me!' A voice carried to Cathy over the sound of the lapping sea. 'What are you doing here?'

Looking for the source of the voice, Cathy struggled to locate it. The voice was a woman's, but as far as she could see, the vast manicured lawn was empty.

'Hello?' Cathy quizzed, as she looked back at the house.

'Up here.' The stern voice commanded.

Cathy caught sight of a woman, not the old woman she had seen from the beach, silhouetted on a balcony high above. It was hard to make out her features as the regal woman remained in the shadows of the eerie house.

'Oh, my!' Her voice changed as Cathy looked up towards the balcony. 'My child, what have you done to yourself. Stay there.'

Before Cathy could protest, the woman disappeared into the house, leaving her confused and alone on the lawn. In a matter of moments, a flurry of movement stole Cathy's attention, and Evie pressed herself against Cathy's leg protectively. Looking towards the side of the house, Cathy felt Evie tense and release a low snarl as the old woman she had seen earlier hobbled around the side of the house and moved towards them.

'Easy girl,' Cathy hushed as she stroked the back of Evie's head.

Cathy watched as the old woman, dressed in all black and aided by a crooked cane, shuffled across the lawn. Rooted to the spot, Cathy looked up to the window and was surprised to see the woman once again shadowed on the balcony. There was something odd about the woman and despite all her effort Cathy could see nothing of her face or features as she remained in the shadows of the house.

'My dear, what has happened to you?' The old woman's voice was hoarse and tarred with an accent Cathy did not recognise. 'Come, come with me and we will get you cleaned up.'

The offer of help snatched Cathy back from the mysterious woman above, and she regained her senses. Suddenly aware that she was in a stranger's garden, being invited into an ominous house by an old woman, she realised it was time to go back to her parents.

'Oh, I'm fine thank you.' Cathy protested as the woman stopped dead in her tracks. 'I should get back to my parents, they're only on the beach.'

'Nonsense.' The old woman snapped. 'I won't allow a young girl to walk the streets as bloodied and messy as you are. Now, follow me and we will see to that cut.'

At the mention of the jagged cut on her forehead, Cathy felt a surge of pain in the injury. In no position to argue, and knowing her family was only on the beach, she grudgingly accepted the old woman's offer and followed her towards the impressive house, with Evie all but glued to her side.

Crossing the lawn, Cathy chanced a glance up towards the balcony and felt relief as the woman was no longer watching her. There was something creepy about her that Cathy couldn't quite place. Brushing the thought aside, she rounded the corner of the house and felt her heart skip a beat.

What she had not been able to see from the beach below was the amazingly crafted sunken courtyard that sat below the level of the lawn. The floor of the sunken courtyard was made of marble, and someone had etched an intricate pattern across the entire surface. Statues sat like chess pieces at sporadic points in the open space, and it was these that stole Cathy's attention.

The statues were like nothing she had seen before, on this side of the mirror. Immediately the style reminded her of Mielikuvitus, as the statues were of fantastically depicted mythical creatures. One statue was something similar to a unicorn, except a pair of wings had been carved from its back, stretching towards its tail.

'Come, don't be afraid.' The old woman cooed as she descended the steps into the courtyard.

Entranced by the statues, Cathy descended the steps and moved to the nearest marble carving. Reaching her hand to the white stone, it surprised her to feel how warm it was to the touch. Tracing her hand across the statue's face, she closed her eyes for a moment.

A memory danced in her mind of her time in Mielikuvitus and the world behind the mirror in her cellar. She remembered the immense city of Partum and the stone table rising high above the city's centre. Forcing her memories to bring to life the creatures of the fantastical world, she struggled to recall the faces of the friends she had made during her time there.

'Is everything ok?'

Opening her eyes, Cathy blushed as the old woman looked at her curiously.

'Yes, sorry. I just think it looks magical.'

'Those things?' The old woman scoffed. 'They were here long before Miss Reine bought the house. I've never been too fond of them.'

'They're amazing.'

The old woman offered a shrug as she retrieved a small first aid box from a table on the far side of the courtyard. Leaving the statue behind her, Cathy moved to join the old woman at the table and pulled out a seat.

'How did you do that, anyway?' The old woman quizzed as she searched through the first aid box.

'I was exploring the rocks and fell over.'

'You wouldn't be the first,' the old woman chuckled. 'I've seen many children take a tumble, I'm sure it's not as bad as it looks.'

Realising she hadn't seen the cut, Cathy looked around for something to see her reflection in, but found nothing. As Evie settled by her side the old woman moved over to her and set about cleaning the blood and grime from Cathy's face.

The courtyard remained uncomfortably silent as Cathy allowed the old woman to sort out her head. Feeling conscious that she was still away from her parents, Cathy tried her best not to look uneasy. Glancing at the woman, she realised she was not as old as she had first appeared. While her posture and shape were haggard and old, her skin seemed younger than it should.

'Ingrid!' The same stern voice bellowed from somewhere inside the mansion house.

'I'm sorry my dear, I'll be back in a moment.' Handing Cathy the bloodstained bandage, the old woman scurried towards the house with the help of her cane.

Taking advantage of the time alone, Cathy dabbed the bandage at her head and was pleased to see no fresh blood staining it. Dropping the bandage to the table, she looked around and saw a shimmer of light reflecting off a tub filled with water.

Moving from her seat, Evie was once again by her side as she walked across to the tub. Again the tub was carved out of the same pale marble as the floor and statues, and while it was filled with water, Cathy could see all the way to the bottom. The still surface of the water gave her enough of a reflection to see the cut above her eye.

'Mum will not be happy with this.' Cathy sighed as she saw a cut stretching from the middle of her eyebrow to her temple. 'Guess Tim will think it looks cool.'

Evie nudged at her leg as she peered into the glassy surface of the water. Something at the bottom of the tub seemed out of place as Cathy leaned closer. At first she thought it had been a trick of light, but as her nose hovered just above the cool surface of the water, there was no denying that something had been painted at the bottom of the tub.

The shape beneath the water was somehow familiar, like something she had seen in a dream. It was the outline that felt familiar; the shape looked like an island in a vast ocean and as she fought to recall where she had seen it before, the sound of footsteps stole her attention.

Unlike Ingrid, the old woman, these footfalls were faster and lighter. Turning around, it surprised Cathy to see a tall woman crossing the courtyard towards her. Turning from the tub, Cathy did not see the water move and take shape as a hand of water had begun to emerge from the surface of the tub. Reaching towards her, the hand was within touching distance when a bark from Evie halted its progress and the hand splashed back into the water.

The woman looked to be in the wrong era and for a ridiculous moment Cathy thought she had been dragged back in time to the Victorian age. The woman wore a regal black dress with a high collar and a hat that's brim was the widest Cathy had ever seen. The hat wafted as the woman walked towards her, and despite hearing her footfalls; the woman seemed to glide over the marble floor towards Cathy and Evie.

'You would do well to allow Ingrid to put a plaster on that.'

The woman's voice was eloquent, well-spoken and very proper. Her narrow lips barely moved as she spoke, and Cathy could only drink in the woman's presence. She looked every part a princess, some member of royalty hiding away in a long forgotten mansion, but Cathy knew that was ridiculous. A few years ago she may have believed this was a princess, but nearly twelve now she was no longer as childish as she had been.

'Thank you.' It was all Cathy could muster as she admired the expensive-looking dress and enormous hat.

'Ingrid tells me your parents are on the beach. I shall send for them to come fetch you.'

'I'll be fine, thank you.' Cathy protested as Evie sat by her leg.

'I won't hear of it.' The woman interrupted before Cathy could add anything more. 'You could easily have a concussion and it would be remiss of me to allow you to walk back to them for fear of hurting yourself again.'

Despite her strange aura, the woman's words were caring enough, and Cathy could tell she would not win the argument. Accepting the offer with a shrug, Cathy watched as the woman span on the spot and returned to the house.

'Ingrid will be out in a moment with a drink and food.'

'Thank you,' Cathy offered as the woman walked through the open door. 'Again.'

Once again alone, Cathy was about to speak to Evie when she realised the woman would not know who her parents were.

'Come on Eevs, I need to tell her where mum and dad are.'

Without a second thought, Cathy raced across the courtyard and up the stairs towards the enormous house on the cliffs.

CHAPTER THREE

SHADOWS AND FACES

Stepping into the vast hallway, Cathy stopped on the threshold to admire the amazing interior of the mansion house. Suits of armour lined the hallway that led to a vast staircase that led up to the upper levels of the house. Display cabinets adorned the walls between the suits of armour, displaying all manner of rarities and antiques.

Evie scanned the wide hallway as they edged deeper into the house and more than once Cathy felt her companion tense as they moved past the armour. Looking to the staircase, Cathy saw that it went up half the level before reaching a landing and dividing into two sweeping staircases that brought you back on yourself.

On the landing, framed between two enormous windows, Cathy saw a large mirror attached to the wall. It resembled the one they had at home, the one she knew had pulled her brother, Tim, to Mielikuvitus. Surrounded by an oversized frame, the mirror was equally, if not more so, ugly than the one that now lived in the secret room in the cellar. Unlike theirs, however, this one had no bird at the top looking down at the glass. This mirror had two skulls, one either side, looking in towards the glass.

'Hello?' Cathy quizzed as she moved along the hallway, conscious she was intruding on the strange woman's privacy. 'Is there anybody there?'

The house was eerily quiet, Cathy's voice echoing up towards the high ceiling. She found no answer from any of the rooms leading off the hallway and returned her attention to the spooky mirror.

Something tickled at her curiosity, and Cathy felt an urge to inspect the mirror. Checking she was still alone and knowing she should take her leave, Cathy tiptoed towards the staircase and made her way to the mirror.

Deep down, she knew it was nothing more than a curious antique. She knew the only passage to Mielikuvitus was locked away in the cellar, but still she wanted to look. Climbing the wide staircase, she noted someone had carved the banister on either side into the shape of hissing snakes, their mouths wide and dead eyes staring towards the open door she had come through.

Admiring the scales along the length of the banister as she moved up, it relieved Cathy to see her own reflection looking back at her from the mirror. Stepping onto the landing, Evie at her side, she moved to stand in front of the tall mirror and admired the ornate skulls on either side.

'And I thought our mirror was ugly,' Cathy scoffed as she looked at the jet-black gems placed in the eye-sockets of the skulls. 'This makes ours look lovely.'

The mirror stood twice as tall as Cathy and as she admired her reflection; she saw how battered and bruised she looked. Her hair was matted with dried blood and seaweed, and her once white t-shirt was stained and torn in a few places.

Admiring the jagged cut above her eye, she leaned closer to the glass to see how deep the cut had been. Although it had stopped bleeding, it was still exposed, and she expected it would leave a scar. Being careful not to start it bleeding again, she groaned at the idea of having her birthday party with an enormous plaster stuck to her forehead.

Cathy was turning twelve in five days, and she was more than a little excited. They had timed their holiday to perfection as they would arrive home the day before her birthday, where her parents had planned a party for her and all her friends. Now, though, she knew she'd forever remember this birthday for the lump and cut on her forehead.

A sudden movement in the reflection snatched her attention back to the moment. In the reflection Cathy was certain she had seen someone on the steps and turned around, expecting to find the regal woman or her elderly helper, but found the staircase empty. As she turned, Evie tensed and once again pressed herself to Cathy's leg protectively.

'Did you see something too?' Cathy hushed to Evie and placed her hand on the nape of the dog's neck.

Certain she had seen movement reflected in the mirror, Cathy inched back to the top step and looked down at the eerie hallway below. Nothing moved, not even the gentle breeze moved the draped fabric hanging from the vaulted ceiling. Although she was alone, Cathy could not shake the feeling she was being watched.

Sensing it was time to go, Cathy looked back at the mirror and as she did, once again she saw a flicker of movement behind her. Snapping her head around a sight that stole her breath and sent a wave of terror shivering down her spine greeted her greeted her.

Beyond the realm of possibility, the two wooden snakeheads were no longer attached to the banister and were now hovering in the air above the bottom step, staring up at her. As their wooden tongues flicked in and out of their now closed mouths, the snakes looked to one another before dropping to the ground and slithering up the staircase towards Cathy.

As the heads moved up the stairs, Cathy saw the wooden body that had been part of the banister was slowly unfurling downwards. Stepping backwards, away from the slithering wooden snakes, Cathy took a position behind Evie, who now snarled at the approaching creatures.

'What are we going to do?' Cathy hushed as she backed away from the top step and looked towards the upper levels of the house.

To Cathy's horror, another pair of wooden snakes moved down the staircases from the upper level of the mansion. She was trapped with nowhere to go expect backing towards the ugly mirror. Feeling her back against the cold glass, Cathy glanced back at the mirror and felt her heart skip a beat in her chest.

Despite being alone on the landing with only Evie by her side, that was not what she saw in the reflection. Staring out of the glass at her was the old woman, Ingrid, dressed in the same weathered clothes, but now with an evil look on her aged face. As Cathy made eye contact with the old woman, something impossible happened.

The old woman in the reflection thrust out her withered hands and Cathy could only watch as they burst through the surface of the mirror, snatching out towards her. Jumping backwards, Cathy almost tripped over Evie, who was still transfixed on the snakes that were now within striking distance.

Cathy's eyes were wide as she watched the old woman climb out of the mirror and move towards her.

'It's time to come with me, little one.' The old woman's voice was no longer soft and caring.

'No.'

'Bring her to me.' The old woman commanded and in response, all four of the snakes attacked at once.

Acting purely on instinct, Cathy ducked down as the first snake launched itself at where she had been standing. Hearing the wooden head crash into the floor, she threw herself over the wooden body and jumped down most of the staircase towards the hallway. Crashing to the floor, she skidded across the tiled floor as Evie released a mighty bark and kept the snakes at bay, giving Cathy a chance to escape.

Struggling to find traction on the slippery tiles, Cathy finally found her footing and launched herself towards the daylight spewing in through the open door. She had made it a half-dozen steps before something blocked her way.

At first Cathy thought it was the regal woman, but in an instant she realised it was a suit of armour that had stepped free of its display plinth. With its sword hanging by its side, the empty armour turned to face her as Cathy skidded to a stop, once again tumbling to the floor. Colliding with the suit of armour's legs, she sent it crashing to the floor but had no time to celebrate as a second and third suit of armour stepped from their positions and closed her down.

Cathy's heart was racing as she cast a glance back to Evie, who was still trapped on the landing above. Preparing to move, Cathy felt cold metal as the nearest suit of armour wrapped its gloved hand around her wrist. Feeling herself hoisted from the ground, Cathy stared into the empty helmet of the armour that now lifted her into the air.

Struggling to break free of the armour's grip, Cathy kicked out with her feet and heard the hollow clang as she kicked the breastplate. Feeling a sting of pain, Cathy heard the old woman's shrill voice barking commands.

'Excellent! Bring her here. Her highness would seek to speak with her.'

'Let me go!' Cathy yelled as the empty armour marched her back towards the sweeping staircase.

The attacking snakes parted to allow the armour passageway, and in the melee, Cathy could see one snake had pinned Evie against the wall beside the mirror. Knowing she was powerless did not stop her from struggling, as Cathy fought with all her strength to break free. Tugging and kicking, she felt a rising sense of dread as she was carried up to the landing and back to the mirror and waiting old woman.

'We have been waiting a long time for you to come.' The old woman sneered as Cathy arrived back on the landing.

'How did you know we would be here?'

'The mirror calls to all of us. You are as powerless to resist its call as we are.'

'Where are you taking me?'

'Back to Mielikuvitus.'

'Why?'

'Because the Dark Queen has commanded it, she has waited a lifetime to seize the strength of a Partum Spiritus and finally see her rise from the shadows.'

'I don't want to go.' Cathy knew her protest sounded childish and ridiculous, but there was little else she could say.

'My child,' the old woman began as she moved to stand in front of Cathy. 'You've longed to return for so long, we've heard your cries in the mirror. Today you get the chance to go back, just as you've been asking.'

Before Cathy could say another word, the old woman took hold of her wrist and placed her free hand against the smooth glass of the mirror.

Cathy was filled with a feeling she had not experienced in a long time and knew she was passing back through the space between two worlds, Although the old woman was right about having longed for the chance to go back, the manner in which she was returning filled her with dread. Nothing about what had happened made her believe that what waited for her on the other side of the mirror would be the happy memories she recalled from her time in Mielikuvitus.

Feeling herself ripped from the landing and transported through the void between the worlds, Cathy closed her eyes and hoped it would not be as bad as she feared. Hearing nothing but her own heart pounding in her ears, Cathy felt the air ripped from her lungs as she crashed to the floor.

Chapter Four

Kingdom Of The Forgottenlands

The floor was cold and much to her relief, solid beneath her. The first thing Cathy could hear was the familiar panting from Evie. Hearing her faithful dog, she opened her eyes and looked around. Evie was on her in a heartbeat, and she felt her rough tongue drag across her cheek, bringing a smile to her face.

'It's going to be ok.'

Cathy nodded and looked around before it sank in what had just happened. Despite trying to take in her surroundings, Cathy realised it had been Evie that had spoken to her.

'How did you, did you just, I mean?' Cathy struggled to form a coherent sentence as her brain raced.

'Talk, yes.'

Cathy looked at Evie dumbstruck as the dog in front of her moved its mouth and spoke again

. Even though she had experienced the fantastical magic of talking creatures when she had been in Mielikuvitus, that had been creatures from there and not a pet from home. Trying to make sense of everything, Cathy was about to speak to Evie again, when the sound of a door opening silenced her.

Turning towards the source of the noise, Cathy saw a barred door open and two figures march through. Cathy and Evie found themselves in a large chamber without windows. The only light came from a bowl of bright blue flames that hung suspended from the ceiling high above them.

Cathy noticed the walls shimmered in the firelight and looked to be made of a mix of dark crystals and stone. Much like she remembered about Mielikuvitus, the walls seemed to have grown from the ground.

'Stand up.' A voice barked from the doorway.

Turning to look at the two guards, Cathy gasped as both creatures removed their oversized helmets to reveal their faces. The only thing Cathy could compare them to were trolls, all bulbous features with oversized bodies and small heads with beady eyes staring at her. They looked ungainly and less than friendly. The one that had spoken sported a matted beard that was tied in a plat beneath its bulbous chin.

'Stay away from her.' Evie snarled and moved to stand between Cathy and the guards.

'Mind your tongue, Hecate, remember your place.' The troll levelled a sword at Evie.

'That's not her name.' Cathy interrupted.

The two trolls erupted into mocking laughter, and Cathy felt her cheeks flush.

'The child knows nothing of our world.' The troll mocked. 'Her highness will make sure you're fully educated about Mielikuvitus.'

'I've been here before.'

As the larger of the two trolls stormed forward and prodded its sword into her back, Cathy had no choice but to follow their lead. Despite Evie's bared teeth, the trolls frogmarched Cathy out of the large cell and out into the walkways of the curious building she was now a prisoner in.

'You may have been to Mielikuvitus before,' the troll continued as they marched along a long corridor. 'But this is the Forgottenlands, a place you will never have visited.'

The name was unfamiliar. In the time she had spent with her family in Mielikuvitus, she had never heard of the Forgottenlands. She knew they had kept her out of a lot of conversations when she had last been here. But even those she had ear wigged on had never mentioned this place. She had been eight when she had last crossed to Mielikuvitus and yet everything felt so different this time around, like somehow it had been more than three years.

Interrupted from her thoughts, they directed Cathy towards a pair of emerald green doors that dominated the end of the corridor. Two more trolls in the same leather and bronze armour stood guard on either side of the doors and snapped to attention as they approached.

'Her highness is expecting you.' One troll barked as they approached.

The doors opened of their own accord and gave Cathy a view into the lavish throne room that sat behind them. The corridor looked drab and uninviting compared to the bright room filled with crystals and fire that was framed by the slowly opening emerald doors.

'Move.' The troll guard behind her barked and pushed Cathy over the threshold into the vast throne room.

'Don't leave me,' Cathy hissed under her breath as she stepped into the throne room.

'I'm not going anywhere, Cathy.' Evie replied, and pressed her fur to Cathy's leg.

Stepping towards the ornate throne on the far side of the room, Cathy took in her surroundings. Everything shimmered and glistened in the same pale blue fire that burned in various bowls and urns around the room. The throne was carved out of the same blue crystal that had been part of the walls in her cell, but someone had polished this to look almost like glass.

On the walls Cathy could make out various paintings and artwork that told a story she did not recognise. Coming to a stop in the centre of the room, Cathy looked at the throne as a tall woman appeared from behind it and stepped into view.

As soon as she saw the woman, Cathy knew it was the same woman from the mansion. There was something about the way she moved, walking whilst seeming to hover above the floor, which gave her away.

'Cathy Scott. Sister of the infamous Timothy Scott and daughter to Partums Susan and Gerard.' Her voice was soft and musical, but laced with a sinister undertone. 'Welcome to my kingdom.'

'Who are you?'

The woman stopped at the side of the throne and for a moment Cathy sensed a frustration in her face.

'You may call me by my inherited title,' the woman hushed. 'I am the Dark Queen of the Forgottenlands.'

The Dark Queen no longer wore the ridiculously oversized hat, and Cathy could see why she had. Her hair was electric blue and her ears were pointed, standing proudly out the side of her head, giving her the look of an elf or fairy. Her face was pale, and the makeup around her eyes matched the vibrant blue of her hair. As Cathy looked closer, it looked as if the Dark Queen's hair was shimmering in the firelight.

The other thing that Cathy noted was the Queen's eyes, her iris' were bright red and highlighted by the pale makeup covering her face. There was, Cathy realised, nothing warm or welcoming about the Dark Queen.

'Why am I here?' Cathy feigned confidence but knew the Queen would see through her attempt to hide her nervousness.

'The time has come for me to seek passage in my purest form to your world.'

'What's that got to do with me?'

'Everything, my dear Cathy, everything.'

As Cathy remained transfixed on the Dark Queen, Evie moved from her side and towards the nearest of the burning bowls of blue fire. Completely ignored by Cathy, Evie moved to the fire and muttered something under her breath into the flames.

'Why didn't you take my brothers, I'm not what they are.'

'That's what makes you so special, young Cathy. Your heart is pure and your connection to the Eternal Flame can be shaped just the way I need.'

The Dark Queen sauntered her way across to stand in front of Cathy. Despite the fear that coursed through her, Cathy remained resolute and firm as the Queen towered over her. Admiring the armoured dress she now wore, Cathy recognised the same snake that had attacked her from the banister etched into the corset-like breastplate. Covering her slender frame, Cathy raised her gaze and admired the collar of black feathers that wafted as she walked.

'I'm not going to help you.'

'You don't have a choice.' The Queen warned as she stroked her fingers across Cathy's cheeks. 'Nobody knows you are here. You are my prisoner and will do as I command if you wish to see your family again.'

Gripping Cathy's chin, the Queen dropped to her haunches to bring her face level with Cathy's. Staring into her red eyes, Cathy could almost see them moving, as if they were made of bubbling lava or fire. She held the Queen's gaze as long as she dared before dropping her eyes to the floor. To her surprise, the Queen held her chin and forced her to look at her face.

'You will do well to do as I command, or see the wrath I can inflict.' The Queen almost whispered the threat as she raised her free hand between them. 'You are not the only one with a connection to the magic of Mielikuvitus.'

Looking at the Queen's hand, Cathy gasped as a ball of water formed in her open palm and took a variety of shapes at the Queen's whispered commands.

'She is not your prisoner!'

The new voice in the throne room stole the Queen's attention as she released her grip on Cathy's chin and span on the spot. Cathy looked towards the source of the voice and smiled as she saw Evie stood by the bowl of burning fire. It had not been Evie that spoke, however, and as she watched, a figure stepped out from the bowl of burning blue fire.

Cathy knew who it was that emerged from the flames. She would recognise his face anywhere. She remembered Sky from her time in Mielikuvitus, and while his beard was peppered with more grey than she remembered, there was no denying it was him.

'Sky!' Cathy beamed as the Elder stalked towards the Dark Queen.

'She is not yours to command, Dark Queen.' Sky warned, and without warning, the Queen attacked.

Using the ball of water in her hand, she launched it at Sky. He was too quick for her attack. Dodging to the side, Sky whipped his fur-lined cloak to the side and caught the rotating orb of water, and threw it back towards her.

Distracted by the defence, the Queen was powerless as Sky launched forward and took hold of Cathy's hand. In a flash of lightning and a crack of thunder, both Cathy and Sky disappeared from the throne room.

'No!' The Queen shrieked as Evie turned to look at her before launching her into the bowl of burning blue flame and disappearing, leaving her alone in the room.

Alone in the throne room, the Dark Queen was furious. Toying with the ball of shimmering water in her hands, her red eyes burned with anger. Without a word, she moved back towards the impressive throne and took her rightful place on the carved seat. Staring out across the now empty room, she could not deny the frustration that boiled inside her.

She had waited for the right moment for decades and now, when all things were just within her grasp, she had allowed her excitement to cloud her perception. The Dark Queen scorned herself for dismissing the Hecate dog that had accompanied Cathy through the mirror. Such a simple oversight and underestimation of Evie had cost the Queen dearly.

Sitting back on the throne, the Queen sighed and closed her eyes for a moment.

'You simply delay the inevitable Elder,' The Queen warned to the empty room. 'I have travelled the same tunnels of the Neverending caves. I know the future holds a place for me in both worlds.'

Chapter Five

Welcome Back

Cathy gasped for breath as she crashed to the floor. Glad to once again feel sand beneath her, she waited for the sound of waves to return. After what felt like an age, the gentle lapping sound filled her ears and she opened her eyes.

'Take a moment.' Sky's familiar voice cooed as Cathy took in her surroundings.

At first she thought she had arrived on the beaches of Halo Cove, but quickly she realised the vast cliffs and rocks were missing. Instead of the vast sheltering of seawater, all she could see was the distant horizon and no sign of land in the distance.

As she stared at the distant horizon, the contrasting hues of blue seemed to move. It dawned on Cathy that the horizon was rocking left and right, rhythmic as if she was moving.

'Where am I?' Her voice was hoarse, dry from the sudden extraction from the Dark Queen's palace.

'Get her a drink,' Sky barked to someone unseen. 'Take your time. You're not used to Beaming, it'll take a few minutes for your body to catch up with itself.'

Grateful for the cup of water that was thrust beneath her face, Cathy snatched it and guzzled down the contents. As she titled her head up to drain the last of the water from the wooden cup, she realised she was looking up at sails.

Her senses returned in a wave of information, as if the water had somehow ignited everything inside her. Rising to her feet, Cathy span a slow circle, taking in the impressive galleon she was now standing on.

Out to one side the vast open seas rolled as far as the eye could see, and on the other were the sandy shores that had been the first thing she had heard. Moving to the edge of the top deck, Cathy looked out towards the land of Mielikuvitus and recognised nothing.

Unlike her memories of Mielikuvitus being vibrant and filled with life and colour, the land beyond the shores was anything but that. Heavy shadows lumbered in the skies, and the landscape looked rough and uninviting. Far off she could see something that resembled a deformed structure and somehow knew, from the sudden churning of her stomach, that was where she had been.

'Welcome back to Mielikuvitus, young Cathy. It has been many years since you last visited.'

'It's been three years.' Cathy corrected as she stared out towards the curious structure. 'Is that where I was?'

'Yes, the Dark Queen's Kingdom. As for the number of years since your last visit, in your world it may have been three but here, it has been far more than that.'

As Sky moved to join her at the deck's edge, Cathy realised how much older he actually looked. When she had glimpsed him as he had emerged from the blue fire, the bright flames had hidden his age. Now, standing in the glorious sunshine reflecting from the choppy sea, his beard was more grey than it had appeared, and his face was more lined than she remembered.

'How long has it been then?'

'Twenty-three years, I fast approach my ninety-ninth birthday.' Sky offered a coy smile, and Cathy could not help but laugh.

'Elder Sky,' a gentle voice interrupted from behind them. 'We are ready to raise anchor.'

'So be it,' Sky replied as he looked out towards the crooked palace. 'The sooner we turn from the Forgottenlands, the better.'

Cathy couldn't agree more. Even turning her back on the foreboding landscape, she could feel the nervousness bubbling in the pit of her stomach. As she was about to speak, Cathy was silenced by the fact the deck remained empty. There was no sign of the person, or creature, that had spoken to Sky not seconds ago.

'Shall we head for Partum?' The voice continued, making Cathy jump back. 'Or would you prefer a more secluded destination?'

'I would seek refuge at Painted Point, if you believe we would be welcomed?'

'As you wish, and of course you will be welcome.'

Cathy could hear footsteps on the wooden decking, but the ship remained empty of anyone but her and Sky.

'What's going on? Where's the person who just spoke to you?'

'I'm right here m'lady.'

'I...' Cathy stammered as she reached out with her hand to where she thought the voice had come from. '...I can't see you.'

Feeling her fingers touch something physical, she quickly retracted her hand.

'Of course you can't,' the voice sighed. 'The daylight is upon me.'

Hearing the footsteps resume, she waited for Sky to offer an explanation. Hearing the anchor being hoisted from the sea, Cathy watched the mainsail unfurl high above her. Turning to watch the pale-pink material catch the wind, she struggled to remain standing as the ship lurched forward.

'Where's Evie?' Cathy asked as she gripped the side rail for support.

'Below deck, waiting for you.'

Sky pointed to a set of ornately carved doors leading beneath the deck of the impressive ship. Grateful to find a distraction, Cathy kept her hold on the railings as she followed sky towards the doors.

'Can I ask you something, Sky?' Cathy pressed, as she tentatively released her grip on the rail and inched to the door.

'You're curious how Evie can speak.'

'Well, yes.' Cathy's nervousness at being aboard the ship was obvious in her quivering voice. 'Does that happen to any animal that comes here?'

Opening the doors, Sky looked strangely uncomfortable as he moved to the side, offering Cathy the stairs. Grateful to leave the deck behind, Cathy gripped the rope and started down the wooden steps.

'Aren't you coming?' Cathy asked, realising Sky had remained at the open doors.

'I need to speak with Captain Flash,' Sky excused. 'Besides, I think Evie has some explaining to do.'

As if on cue, Cathy sensed movement at the bottom of the steps and turned to see Evie pad into a pool of light from the open doors. Looking up from below deck, Evie's ears were back, and there was sadness to her normally jubilant and playful expression.

'We should talk.' Evie offered, her slender snout moving as she spoke. 'I don't want you to be mad at me.'

'Why would I be mad?'

Without offering an answer, Evie moved deeper into the hold of the ship and Cathy could only follow. As Sky closed the doors behind her, it plunged her into darkness for a second until something bathed the hold in a pale light.

In the centre of the room, Evie stood beneath a flickering lamp that hung from the underside of the deck. The fire flared, and it was the only source of light that allowed Cathy to see. The hold was clearly a sleeping area for the invisible crew as hammocks swung between the support struts holding the heavy deck in place above.

'What's going on, Eevs?'

'Come and sit down, I'll tell you everything.'

Weaving her way through the maze of hammocks, Cathy found a seat on an upturned barrel and waited for Evie to speak. Unsure if they were alone, Cathy realised she had never been aboard a ship before.

Giving Cathy a moment to admire the craftsmanship of the impressive galleon, Evie hesitated in offering Cathy her explanation. Seeing her wide eyed and filled with wonder, she knew it would upset Cathy when she heard the truth.

'I'm not from your world, Cathy.' Evie confessed, as Cathy snatched her head around to stare at her. 'I am a Hecate, born free in the lands around the Eternal Lake.'

'No,' Cathy interrupted. 'I remember mum and dad bringing you home as a puppy.'

'They chose me to be by your side, remaining as your protector and connection to Mielikuvitus.'

'That's not how it works,' Cathy protested, her mind swimming with a million thoughts. 'Tim has an Ecilop, so does Aiden.'

'Every Partum is assigned a protector. For centuries, that honour has fallen to the Ecilop. But with you, Cathy, your spirit connected with Mielikuvitus differently.'

'What do you mean?'

'When you were taken by the Minotaur of the mountains.'

'Minnie!' Cathy corrected. 'Her name was Minnie.'

'I'm sorry, Minnie. When she took you from your family, she became your ally in our world. Because of this, the Ecilop refused to replace her, honouring the sacrifice she made in the battle against the Dark Entity.'

'But you've never spoken to me before.'

'When I agreed to live by your side, it was on the condition I play my part in silence. Adhering to the rules of your world.'

'But you could talk if you'd wanted to?'

The hurt was obvious on Cathy's face as she recalled all the times she had sat alone and shared everything with Evie. There wasn't a thing Cathy had not shared with Evie in the last three years. There was no secret she had kept from her, and suddenly she felt betrayed. One memory, more vivid than all others, came flooding back to her.

'Why didn't you talk to me when I needed a friend?' Cathy's eyes filled with tears. 'When Grandma Lily died, I was alone and needed you.'

'I listened.'

'But you could have made it all better. You could have told me it wouldn't hurt forever. Didn't you want to talk?'

'More than anything I wanted to help, whisper in your ear that I would always be by your side.' Evie dropped her gaze to the floor. 'It was forbidden and they would have taken me from you.'

'That's not fair.'

'No, it wasn't.' Evie agreed, as she moved to sit in front of Cathy. 'But now we are here, now we can be free to speak.'

'I need some time.'

Placing her paw on Cathy's knee, Evie looked into her eyes and offered a nod.

'I understand, just know that I have only ever been by your side and will always be with you.'

'I know.' Cathy wiped the tears from her cheeks. 'I just need to think about things for a while.'

'I'll wait for you here.'

As Cathy rose from her seat, Evie's sad eyes followed her back towards the staircase. Not moving from where she was sat, Evie remained sullen and silent until Cathy had left the hold.

Emerging back onto the deck, Cathy felt betrayed by everyone. Deep down she felt an anger towards her parents and while she could, in some way, understand why they had done what they had, it still hurt. Moving to the back of the ship, Cathy wasn't sure if she was alone but as she let the tears fall down her face, she didn't care.

Chapter Six

Captain Flash

With the galleon underway, Cathy emerged on the deck and felt the force of the air whipping past her face. Grateful to have tied her hair in a ponytail, it surprised her how fast the ship was moving and how little motion she felt.

When they had been anchored on the shores of the Forgottenlands, the ship had been rocking back and forth and now, despite their speed, the ship was holding steady. Looking around, she saw rigging ropes and equipment moving around the deck, moved by the invisible creatures that had spoken to Sky.

'Why doesn't it surprise me?' Cathy hushed to herself as she moved towards the enormous wheel on the top deck.

'M'lady,' a voice greeted as she climbed towards the ship's wheel.

'Oh, hello.'

'Proud to have you aboard the Lady Chance.'

The voice was coming from the side of the large wooden wheel and Cathy suspected, if it were visible, she would see someone steering the ship in whichever direction they intended. It was a strange voice, hard to distinguish an accent, but whoever spoke, enunciated the letter 'r' as they spoke, almost rolling it over their invisible tongue.

'Where are we going?'

'Far from the Forgottenlands M'lady,' the voice responded. 'Elder Sky would seek you far from the reaches of the Dark Queen.'

'Where is he?'

'Sky?'

'Yes.'

'He's watching from the ship's head.'

'The what?'

'The front M'lady, you'll find him scanning the seas ahead.'

Thanking the jolly voice, Cathy made her way back to the deck and towards the front of the large galleon. Catching sight of Sky, she made her way to him and joined him on a small raised platform overlooking the front of the ship.

Cathy was about to announce her arrival when she chanced a glance down towards the water. Expecting to see the sea crashing against the wooden hull of the ship, she was dumbstruck as she saw the ship was actually hovering above the surface of the water.

The barnacle covered hull was proud of the sea's surface, as if the ship were in fact hovering above the turbulent sea.

'How?' Cathy gasped as she leant over the waist-high edge of the main deck.

'Careful,' Sky sighed as he took hold of her shoulder to pull her back. 'If you were to fall, the speed of the Lady Chance would see you far from rescue in a matter of seconds.'

'What is going on, Sky?' Cathy asked, her attention still fixed on the impossibly flying ship.

The Lady Chance was a galleon of immense size and grandeur. Much akin to the ships of old, the Lady Chance had two main masts and a vast array of sails that trapped the wind and propelled them forward. The outer hull was made of polished wood and inlaid with veins of silver and gold.

Looking at the vessel, it was apparent the ship was one of war. Fortified armour had been strategically attached on various elements of the hull. As it hovered above the surface of the Eastern Sea, the ship had a single rudder slicing through the water beneath the centre of the hull. Propelled by the wind, the ship glided through the air with ease, leaving only the faintest of trails in its wake.

'Are we flying?'

'Not quite,' Sky chortled as he let Cathy take in the curious movement of the floating ship. 'The Lady Chance is a cleverly crafted ship, one of very few remaining in Mielikuvitus. Her design is one that allows us to move with the help of the wind and maintain a position just above the surface of the sea.'

'Why?'

'So many questions, I can tell you're related to Timothy!' Cathy blushed as Sky grinned. 'The Thunders perfected the art of wind-sailing many years ago, it's all down to the design of the ships and the sails.'

'The design of the ship?'

'Follow me.' Sky chuckled and led Cathy to a narrow platform that circled around the entire outer hull.

Barely wide enough for them to walk along, Cathy was nervous. The only thing stopping her from tumbling into the sea were two lengths of rope that acted as the barrier between her and certain death. Keeping her hand on the outer hull, she followed close behind Sky as he walked along the length of the Lady Chance.

With the wind whipping past them, Sky had to raise his voice to be heard.

'The ships are made of a series of hollow pipes that filter the wind through and into the rudder. The sails drag us forward and the air that is caught in the pipes pushes us ever faster through the sea.'

Reaching the front of the ship, further forward than where they had been stood on the deck, Cathy looked up and saw a honeycomb of tube openings stretching the height of the ship. Standing so close she could hear the wind whistling along the tubes and around the length of the ship. It was a curious feeling as the wind whipped the front of the hull, Cathy felt like it was dragging her towards the array of holes.

'Where are you taking me?'

'The Painted Point.'

'Not Partum City, or Poc?'

'You remember them?' Sky beamed as he turned to look at her.

'How can I forget them? I've been wanting to come back since the moment we left.'

'It wasn't your time.' Sky sighed. 'It still isn't your time, you shouldn't be here.'

'Why am I here then?'

'The Dark Queen.' Sky hung on the name for a moment. Cathy could see the change in his expression. 'She has been growing in power for many years. She has her reasons for luring you back through the mirror, and right now I'm not entirely sure why.'

'I don't think it was for anything good.' Cathy remarked, her knuckles white as she gripped the rope. 'She wasn't exactly nice to me. Who is she?'

'Judging by the look on your face, maybe we should return up deck and continue my explanation there?'

Cathy was all too eager to accept Sky's offer and promptly followed him back onto the main deck. When a more substantial edge again protected her from falling into the sea, she looked around the deck and realised the sun was starting to set.

'Well timed.' Sky smiled. 'It is time you met our generous host and captain of the Lady Chance.'

As the sun descended, it painted the sky in a hue of red and gold. The shadows of the mast and sails covered the deck, and Cathy watched as the captain appeared out of thin air beside the enormous wheel.

What she saw caught her completely by surprise, but explained why the voice had been rolling the letter 'r' in every word. While the figure beside the wheel looked human in its shape, its head anything but human. Instead of the familiar face, the ship's captain had the head of a tabby cat, complete with whiskers and a collection of golden earrings pierced into his left ear.

'Pleasure to make your acquaintance, M'Lady.' The captain offered as he stepped away from the wheel to stand at the top of the steps.

Cathy took a moment to admire the ship's captain as he stood above her. Dressed in typical pirate clothing, it was almost comical to be looking at the human-cat. He wore a waistcoat that was too small for him and carried a trio of swords to one side, attached to a large-buckled belt.

'You can call me Cathy. I don't like being called M'Lady, it sounds like something someone would call my mum.'

The captain's face dropped, and the flamboyance evaporated from his posture. Pouncing from where he stood, the captain somersaulted through the air and landed on the deck in front of Cathy. Dropping to one knee, the captain lowered his head and placed a pawed hand on Cathy's.

'I offer my most humble apologies. Please accept them. I meant no offence to you at all.'

Looking down at the cat, she glanced at Sky, who fought to hide a smile on his bearded face.

'You are like royalty to them. They worship the Partum Spiritus and the thought of offending you is terrifying to him.'

'Oh no, I didn't mean that I was offended.' Cathy pleaded and tugged at the captain's hand to get him to stand up. 'Please, stand up.'

Tugging at his soft paws, Cathy encouraged the humbled feline captain to stand. Once they were face-to-face, Cathy could see he was reluctant to meet her gaze and kept his shimmering blue eyes looking towards the wooden deck.

'My name is Captain Flash, this is my ship the Lady Chance. My crew and I, are honoured to transport the Partum Spiritus wherever she may need to go.'

'Well, Captain Flash, you can call me Cathy and I'm very grateful for your help.'

As Cathy lifted Captain Flash's chin, forcing him to look at her, it surprised her how soft his fur was to her touch. For a moment the cat captain struggled to meet her gaze, but when he did, a silent exchange saw his flamboyant attitude return.

'The setting sun allows me and my crew to appear before you.' Flash announced as he licked a paw and swept back his ears. 'I should introduce you to the Lady Chance's crew.'

A sudden chorus of meows carried over the whistling wind and Cathy turned to see they now filled the deck with cat-like creatures, like Flash. She could see every type of fur she could imagine, ginger, black, striped, spotted, mottled and others she would never have seen back home. Cats of every shape and size littered the deck, but it was a rotund, grey-haired cat that caught her attention through the crew.

The grey crewmate offered her a coy smile as it stood twice the size of all the others. Larger and fatter, the lumbering cat raised a mop into the air in celebration of the captain's introduction.

'We are Thunders, conquerors of the seas and masters of the wind.' Flash announced with immense pride. 'Tonight, by the pale moon, we shall celebrate and feast. In the morning we will arrive at Painted Point.'

Before Cathy could answer, the deck became a hive of activity, with crewmates scattering in every direction. Astounded by what she was looking at, Cathy caught sight of Evie peering through the double doors leading to the lower decks. Although she still felt betrayed by Evie's silence back home, she understood the reasons.

'I need to speak with Evie.' Cathy hushed to Sky, who offered a simple nod of agreement.

'Make your peace with her. She has and always will be, your greatest friend and ally.'

Knowing Sky was right, Cathy made her way back to the double doors to make amends with Evie.

CHAPTER SEVEN

MOONLIGHT FEAST

Cathy and Evie spent the early part of the evening on the front deck, watching the blanket of stars flicker to life. Above the sound of the feline crew, Cathy had enjoyed the sounds of the sea crashing into the narrow wooden blade that held them above the surface of the water. At first the pair had sat in silence. That silence had soon been broken when Cathy had offered her friend an apology.

With the awkward air between them cleared, Cathy had launched a flurry of questions at Evie, who was more than excited to answer. With her legs dangling between the struts of the railings, Cathy listened intently to every word that Evie spoke.

Before she had realised, the sun had completely disappeared and been replaced by a waxing moon that looked nothing like the one she was used to. Unlike the familiar moon of our world, the moon in Mielikuvitus shone a pale purple. Painting the world in its light, Cathy noticed there were no craters, and the surface appeared smooth and unblemished.

'Might I interrupt for a moment?' Sky asked as he approached from behind.

'Of course. Is dinner ready? I'm starved.' Cathy replied, as she dragged her feet back from between the wooden railings.

'Not quite,' Sky offered with a grin. 'Perhaps Evie here can check with Captain Flash and see how much longer we have to wait?'

Understanding the hint, Evie nuzzled her damp nose against Cathy's cheek and padded off across the deck, leaving them alone. Bathed in the purple hue of the moonlight, Cathy looked at Sky and took in his appearance.

The Elder was exactly as she remembered, if only a little older. Dressed in the brown fur-lined cape, she recalled having seen Sky in his dog form. Despite all that had happened, it suddenly dawned on her that Evie and Sky shared the same origins in their animal form.

'Can Evie do what you do?'

'I beg your pardon.'

'I mean, change into a human, like you can?'

'I'm afraid not. While we may look the same, our species are very different to one another, where Evie is a Hecate, I am not.' Cathy was about to press further, but Sky altered the course of the conversation with ease. 'I had wanted to get you home without a need to give you this, but I fear that would be a naïve hope.'

Removing something from beneath his robe, Cathy looked at the wrapped item in his hand. Wrapped in a sheet of brown cloth and sealed with leather, Sky offered her whatever it was. Awash with curiosity, Cathy took the item and felt a strange warmth from beneath the fabric as she took it in her hand.

'What is it?'

'Open it, and hopefully you'll remember.'

Bathed in the moonlight, Cathy untied the leather twine and unwrapped the item. As soon as the moonlight shimmered off the carved stone, she knew what it was she had been given. Recognising the carved head of a jaguar, she quickly exposed the entire weapon and looked at the dragon's head on the opposite end.

'I can't remember what it's called.' Cathy confessed as she held the weapon in front of her face.

Fighting to recall its name, Cathy remembered what she had seen her family do with their own weapons. She had seen her mum and dad call the fire from their own carved weapons, and even Tim had used his own to fight back against the Dark Entity.

'Aralcym.' Sky hushed as he pointed to the Jaguar's head.

'You were much smaller when you last held it in your hand. I recall your fingers barely able to wrap around the handle.' Sky mused as he rolled Cathy's fingers around the bound handle between the stone heads. 'Now, it is a very different sight.'

'I don't even know what to do with it.'

'I will show you once we arrive at Painted Point. For now, I thought its best place was in your hands.'

'Thank you, I think.'

'Come, I expect the feast will be ready by the time we get below deck.' Pausing, Sky looked at Cathy for a moment. 'I think we should see you changed into more appropriate clothes.'

Accompanying Cathy into the bowels of the ship, neither of them saw the feint light in the water behind them. A trio of flickering lights kept pace with the fast-moving ship as it skimmed across the surface of the

Eastern Sea. Unaware they were being followed, Cathy and Sky descended into the ship's bowels.

It didn't take long for Cathy to get changed into the clothes that had been set aside for her. Slipping the royal blue dress over her head, she was relieved to see they had not dressed her in the strange side-cape clothes that she remembered her brothers having to wear when she had been here last. Straightening the skirt down her legs, she admired her reflection in a polished mirror.

'It's not like the clothes you made Tim wear.' Cathy declared as she emerged from the small room. 'What's with that?'

'The clothes your brothers wore were more formal attire. This is something far more practical and appropriate. Wouldn't you agree?'

Cathy nodded as she rubbed her hand along the folded fabric that made up the dress. It was a strange feeling, not what she expected, as the fabric felt smooth and yet rough at the same time. Once again, much like the Aralcym she had been given, the clothes felt warm to the touch.

'There's one thing missing.' Evie announced as she padded down the staircase into the room.

'What's that, Eevs?'

On cue, Sky retrieved a narrow leather belt from a table at his side. Standing in front of Cathy, he hooked it around her waist and fastened the ornate silver clasp together. Straightening the lower part of the dress, Sky held out his hand and waited for Cathy to hand him the Aralcym.

'Always carry it by your side.' Sky hushed as he hooked the Aralcym onto the belt. 'That way, the

Eternal Flame will always be with you, should you need it.'

'They're ready for us.' Evie announced, offering Cathy a look of approval.

Knowing there were a million questions she wanted to ask, Cathy knew now was not the time. Taking Sky's lead, they once again returned to the main deck and the sight that greeted them stole Cathy's breath.

The entire main deck had been transformed into an open dining area. Two fire pits roared at either end of the deck while four tables had been set out in a trident shape facing to the front of the ship. Food was being cooked over each of the fire pits while the majority of the crew were sitting along the lengths of the tables.

'Ah, Cathy Scott.' Captain Flash announced, his voice slurring just enough to tell her he had partaken in some drinking in her absence. 'Come join me at the head table, this feast is in your honour.'

Grateful that the moonlight was blocked out by a cover of sheets that had been erected between the masts, Cathy could hide the embarrassment that flushed her face. Feeling every set of eyes on her, Cathy fought to maintain her composure as she made her way to join Flash at the head table.

'Thank you,' The merry captain grabbed Cathy and hugged her.

'Come, sit.' Flash exclaimed and thrust a wooden cup into Cathy's hand.

Taking her seat, she was glad that Sky moved to sit beside her and even more glad when he slid the wooden cup away from her. Leaning close, the Elder whispered in her ear so the eager ship's captain could not hear them.

'Even in Mielikuvitus you're too young to partake in the drinking of wine.'

'Good.' Cathy chortled. 'I just wanted a normal drink.'

Waving his hand over the top of the cup, Cathy watched with astonishment as the liquid content evaporated. Once the cup was empty, the cup was filled with a pale mist that tumbled over the lip of the cup. Raising it to his nose, Sky took a long sniff up and, seeming to be satisfied with what he had created, handed the cup to Cathy.

'Oh, come now, Sky.' Captain Flash exclaimed. 'Let the girl drink, she's our honoured guest.'

'It's fine,' Cathy protested, taking a sip of the bubbling liquid. 'I'm fine with this.'

The taste of the drink was like nothing Cathy had ever tasted before. It was as if Sky had infused every single flavour she had ever tasted in the bubbling liquid. Her taste buds exploded with delight as she gulped down the contents and before Cathy returned the cup to the tabletop, it had refilled itself.

'How?' Cathy gasped as she looked at Sky.

'Let an old man have his secrets.' Offering her a playful wink, Captain Flash announced the start of the feast.

'My fearless crew, my friends and my kin.' Captain Flash slurred. 'Tonight we dine beneath the stars in the presence of a true Partum Spiritus. Never has such an honour been bestowed upon the Lady Chance and I would see her well fed.'

Slamming his hand down onto the table, Cathy was once again speechless as the tables became filled with food that threatened to overflow onto the deck below.

'Wow!' Was all she could muster.

'Eat, celebrate and be merry.'

Dropping back into his seat, the crew needed no further invitation. In an instant, the tables were filled with excited chatter and raised voices as the crew dived into the piles of food spread across the tables.

Seeing the crew eating, Cathy realised how hungry she was. Not recognising the plethora of food in front of her she tentatively filled her plate with things she thought she would like. Before long, Cathy found herself as eager as those around her to make her way through the vast array of food.

The feast and celebrations stretched into the night and before long Cathy's eyes were heavy with tiredness as she slumped in her seat. Allowing herself to drift into dreams. The last thing she remembered was a strange display of acrobatics by one of the crew as they danced and jumped between the three tables.

Cathy had longed to return to Mielikuvitus for so long, and now she was here. It was everything she had remembered and more. With a smile on her face, she allowed her eyes to close and sleep to swallow her.

Her dreams, however, were not as welcoming as her reception in Mielikuvitus. That night, they were plagued with visions of the Dark Queen and an unshaking feeling that she had not seen the fearsome woman for the last time.

CHAPTER EIGHT

AMBUSH

Cathy awoke with a start as the ship rocked violently. Thrown from her bed, she crashed to the wooden floor. Evie jumped to her feet as the sound of an explosion echoed from outside.

'What's happening?' Cathy groaned as she searched around for the Aralcym she had placed on the end of her bed.

'I'm not sure.' Evie's ears twitched as another explosion shook the ship. 'Whatever it is, it can't be good.'

Once the ship stopped rocking, Cathy launched to the door and sprinted up towards the deck. Evie was hot on her heels as she pushed through the door to be met with a sight that stole her breath.

The crew were once again invisible in the sunlight, but she saw their shapes as the waves crashed over the sides of the ship as another explosion erupted out of the water. Seeing the water create the outline of the feline crew, Cathy looked beyond the magical sight to the trio of ships that bobbed in the water behind the Lady Chance.

The ships differed from the Lady Chance and looked at odds with all she had seen in Mielikuvitus. They looked a perverse mixture of Mielikuvitan organic construction and some modern warship from home. Angular and imposing, the three ships remained a distance back as the central ship fired another barrage towards them.

Cathy felt herself shoved to the side as the cannonball hurtled towards the ship and smashed through the deck where she had been standing. Showered with splinters of wood, she turned to see it was Sky that had pushed her out of harm's way.

'Who are they?' She gasped, wiping the wood from her hair.

'The Dark Queen's navy.' Sky hissed, his eyes narrowing as he watched the three ships move closer.

'How didn't we see them before?'

'They glide beneath the surface of the water until they attack.'

'Like submarines?'

Cathy saw the look of confusion on Sky's face, but had no chance to react as Captain Flash's familiar voice bellowed from the top deck.

'They move to attack on both sides.' It filled his voice with frustration and while Cathy couldn't see him, she could tell the expression that would be painted on his face. 'Hold us steady, drop the side sails and slow us down.'

'But, captain.' another voice shrieked. 'If we slow, they'll be on us in a heartbeat.'

'Do as you're told.'

Cathy watched as the furthest sails that hung over the sides of the ship were collapsed and tied back against the short crossbeams. With the lower sails no longer catching the wind, the ship's momentum slowed. Still catching the wind, they remained raised out of the water on the narrow blade that dissected the waves, but no longer moved with haste.

'What's he doing?'

Seeing the sleek and imposing ships gain on them, Cathy could not help but feel a rising sense of dread.

'Can you remember how to use that?' Sky snapped as he snatched the Aralcym from her side.

'No.'

'You will!' His voice was firm as he watched the two ships separate to flank either side of the Lady Chance. 'If they board the ship, do not let yourself be taken.'

Giving Cathy no chance to reply, Sky sprinted across the deck and to where Cathy presumed Flash to be. Moving to the railing, Cathy watched as the nose of the attacking ships passed along the length of the Lady Chance. Although they had looked imposing at a distance, seeing the shimmering black surface of the ships so close sent a shudder down her spine. Seeming to be carved out of smoked glass, the ships sliced through the water with ease.

'Captain!'

'Hold her steady.'

'But Captain...'

'Bite your tail, hold her steady.'

Cathy watched as the two ships moved in unison to either side of the Lady Chance. Unlike the invisible crew, she could see the plethora of armoured trolls, like the guards in the Dark Queen's palace, gathered on the deck. Dressed in armour and holding spears and shields, they looked terrifying.

'This can't be the right choice.' She hushed at Evie, who remained by her side. 'Why are we letting them close us down? Surely we can go faster with all those sails?'

Looking up at the vast array of pink-fabric sails whipping in the wind, she felt that Flash was making the wrong choice. Watching every move of the trolls, Cathy shrieked as the ship in front of her now faced them with a side of exposed cannons protruding from the hull.

'Hold.' Flash barked as they all watched the attacking ships.

Cathy held her breath, seeing the flicker of flames in the shadowy recess behind the cannons, she knew the crews were preparing to fire. Even a quick scan of the other ship told her there were over thirty cannons pointed at the Lady Chance and she knew the same would happen behind her.

'Captain?'

'Fire!' The command came not from Flash, instead it carried across the waves from the ship in front of Cathy.

'Collapse all sails and block the hollows.'

As the crew responded, Cathy felt her stomach lurch as the Lady Chance dropped back into the water. With the tubes now blocked, the air no longer fed through the wooden blade and held them above the sea's surface. In a split second they dropped back into the water, and at the same time the attacking ship fired.

A wall of cannonballs flew towards where the Lady Chance had been. With the ship no longer raised from the water, only a handful of the cannonballs smashed through the masts of the ship, the rest continued their flight through the air.

Catching sight of the mass of metal balls, Cathy followed them and watched as they ripped through the hull of the ship on the opposite side. A cacophony of explosion ripped through the air as the outer hull of the second ship was torn apart by the barrage of cannonballs.

'FIRE!' This time the command came from Flash.

In response, the Lady Chance unleashed her own barrage of cannons towards the attacking ship and Cathy watched the hull become peppered with flaming holes. Screams of delight erupted on the deck, and Cathy felt herself swell with relief as the two ships sank beneath the surface of the water.

Cathy's celebration was short-lived as the cries of victory were silenced by a shrill voice somewhere towards the back of the Lady Chance.

'Prepare for boarding.'

Cathy snatched her head around to see the third ship taking advantage of the sudden distraction. Bearing down on them, Cathy saw the crew of trolls waiting on the ship's front as it closed the gap between them with frightening pace.

'Drop sail, open the hollows and prepare for attack.'

Feeling the Lady Chance once again lift from the surface of the sea, Cathy knew it was too late. The prow of the third black ship collided with the rear of the Lady Chance and Cathy watched as a dozen well-armed trolls swung through the air towards her.

Gripping the Aralcym in her hand, Cathy screamed as two trolls landed on the deck to her side. In a heartbeat, Evie launched an attack on the nearest troll, leaving Cathy alone with the second of the armoured creatures. Gripping the bound handle, Cathy's heart pounded in her chest as she willed something to happen.

The troll did not wait. Seeing its prize, it moved to grab Cathy, but she quickly dodged the oversized hand stretching towards her. Slamming the stone dragon's head into the troll's hand, Cathy longed for the flame to burst from the mouth as she remembered her brother's weapons doing. Despite her willing it, the Aralcym remained lifeless in her hand.

Hearing Evie yelp, she chanced a glance at her companion and grinned as she saw the troll drop onto the deck, unmoving. Distracted by the sound, Cathy felt a solid blow crash into the side of her head as her own attacker moved to strike.

Flying through the air, Cathy crashed to the deck and collided with the motionless body that Evie had bested. Crashing into the armoured body, she felt the air ripped from her lungs. Sensing the second troll bearing down on her, and seeing more swinging from the attacking ship, she looked around for something to use.

Seeing the sword in the dead troll's hand, Cathy ripped it free and raised it above her as the second troll towered over her. The sword was heavy in her hands, and she almost lost her grip as the troll smashed his own blade into hers. Fighting against the sudden force, Cathy did her best to hold back her attacker.

Unable to get up, Cathy scrambled over the dead troll as blow after blow rained down at her. Casting aside what she could, her heart pounded in her eyes, and the world around her swam with fear.

'Cathy Scott!' The voice was cold and familiar.

Standing proudly on the bowsprit of the attacking ship, Cathy could see the Dark Queen staring down at her. In the sunlight her blue hair shimmered like a demonic halo around her head. Still dressed in the curiously armoured dress, she now held a weapon similar to Cathy's in her slender hand.

'Get away from her.' Evie snapped as she intercepted an unseen attack from the troll that Cathy had been fighting.

'Give me the girl or I shall send your beloved ship to the depths of the Eastern Sea.'

The Dark Queen's voice hung in the air after she had finished speaking and Cathy watched as a snake of blue flame crept from the end of the Dark Queen's weapon.

'She is a Partum,' Sky announced as he sprinted across the deck to Cathy's side. 'Cathy is not yours to claim.'

'Step aside, Elder. Your time is passed.' The Dark Queen spoke with frightening menace. 'It is my time to reign, as my mother would have seen if you had not interfered.'

'I still live with the consequences of your mother's sins.'

'As do I.'

Cathy watched the snaking blue flame as it wound its way down the front of the Dark Queen's ship towards the Lady Chance.

'Unfurl and fly.' Captain Flash declared, and in an instant, all sails opened and caught the wind.

The Lady Chance lurched forward and Cathy watched as they ripped free from Queen's attacking ship. As they moved away, Cathy saw the queen raise her hand to give command to pursue but watched in astonishment as Sky snatched the Aralcym from her hand and pointed it towards the Dark Queen.

In Sky's hands, the weapon reacted as a ball of fire erupted with a sickening shriek and spewed outwards at the Dark Queen. Responding with her own weapon, Cathy watched as the snaking blue flames fought to hold back the fire Sky had launched, to no avail. Crashing into the ship's front, Cathy watched as the flames consumed the shimmering hull.

Expecting to see the Dark Queen flee, Cathy watched as the regal woman walked through the flames to perch on the very tip of the bowsprit. Her face was twisted into a venomous snarl, and Cathy could feel her glare burning into her. Over the roar of the flames Cathy was sure she heard the Dark Queen speak, but could not make sense of the words. Despite this, she could tell her meaning by the evil look on her face.

With the ship disabled, they made quick progress away from the attack, and Cathy watched as the burning ship soon became less obvious in the sea behind them.

'We have much work to do,' Sky sighed as he handed Cathy her Aralcym. 'You should not find yourself without an answer from the Eternal Flame. You should be ready next time.'

'Next time?'

'The Dark Queen will not stop until she has you.' Sky's face was filled with concern. 'I fear there may be only one way to get you home and you are nowhere near ready for that.'

'What?'

'We will worry about that later,' Sky replied as he turned away from the fading silhouette of the Dark

Queen's ship. 'We should make the Painted Point before nightfall. Once there, we shall begin your training.'

Leaving Cathy and Evie alone on the deck, Sky descended the stairs into the lower decks. As he moved, Cathy could see how much energy it had taken to call the flame from her Aralcym. Admiring the stone carvings, she feared such control and power were far beyond her own capabilities.

Chapter Nine

Painted Point

With no sign of the Dark Queen's ship in pursuit, Cathy watched the sun creep towards the horizon as they neared the coastline. In the distance she could make out plumes of smoke and, as the sky became darker, Captain Flash announced their arrival at Painted Point.

Much to Cathy's disappointment, Painted Point was nothing like she had expected. Remembering the grand appearance of Partum City, this was anything but. As the Lady Chance slowed her pace and crept towards the docks, all Cathy could see was a shanty town.

Painted Point looked like some ancient pirate settlement that she had seen in history books at school. Plumes of smoke billowed from the open spaces between the wooden structures. None of the dwellings matched. Everything seemed to be built in the preferred design of whoever had constructed it, with no care for uniformity.

'What's with this place?' Cathy quizzed as Flash navigated the enormous ship towards the docks.

'It's my home.' Flash yelled from the top deck.

As the sun dipped below the horizon, night's arrival allowed Flash to once again take appearance in front of her. Seeing the excitement on his feline face made her take another look at the dilapidated city.

Seeing the strange wooden town, Cathy caught sight of a group of children playing in an open courtyard. Some looked to be the same species as Flash, while others in the group looked a mix of different races she had never seen.

'We will be docked in a minute, I'll be glad to be off the ship.' Evie nuzzled against Cathy as she placed her front paws on the side of the ship.

As the ship approached the dockside, a crowd had gathered. Moving closer, Cathy could hear the excited chatter amongst the gathered faces. Scanning the crowds, she saw many faces similar to Flash's, including one elderly looking feline that stood ahead of the crowd.

'Bubus-anjam will meet you when we disembark.' Sky declared as he moved to join Cathy.

'Who's that?'

'He is Painted Point's captain. He oversees the town and what it stands for.'

'What does it stand for?'

'It's a haven for those without a place to call home. His kind, the Thunders, have always lived at sea but there is always a need to find a home on land.'

'Why do they call him a captain if he lives on the land?'

Sky couldn't help but chuckle at Cathy's questioning. He could see so much of Timothy in her, and yet Cathy was very much her own person. Looking at Cathy, Sky could see the thirst for knowledge and understanding and was in no mood to disappoint. As the crew of the Lady Chance bustled around them, Sky offered Cathy a potted history of Painted Point.

'Painted Point is a moving place. If you look beyond the strange structures, you will see we haven't really hit land.'

Cathy turned her attention back to the town, and she realised what Sky was saying. Despite looking like a city built on land, the sea was still lapping beneath the mishmash of streets made of wood. There was, now that she looked closer, no sign of soil or ground anywhere as she could see.

'How is that possible?'

'Painted Point is a floating town, always hugging the coast of the Eastern Sea. She flows with the current and is always moving to keep the people safe.'

'Why don't they find somewhere on land?'

'Many centuries ago, the Thunders lived in the Forgottenlands until they destroyed their homes to make way for the Croinsop. Do you remember them?'

The memory of the fearsome part-scorpion creatures that had marched for the Dark Entity raced through her mind. She had never confessed to her parents that the Croinsop had been the source of many nightmares as she had grown up and their terrifying appearance haunted her more than she would confess to anyone. Wanting to move on from the memory, Cathy offered a nod as she kept her attention fixed on the amazing floating town.

'I remember them.' She answered, her voice betraying the sense of fear she tried to keep hidden.

'With the invasion of the Forgottenlands, the Thunders took to the seas and have remained there ever since.'

'Didn't they try to take it back?'

'The Thunders do not seek conflict, they are mostly a peaceful people and only fight to protect themselves. It is not in their nature to seek out battle.'

'I don't understand that,' Cathy mused as the Lady Chance dropped anchor. 'Why wouldn't you take back what is yours if someone has taken it from you? Surely that's wrong.'

'Maybe you can ask Bubus-anjam why he chose to keep his people moving. Of course, if they had returned to the Forgottenlands I expect the Dark Queen would have laid waste to their people in the end. I fear a life always on the move was their safest choice.'

'Sky, you old dog!'

The grey-furred feline bellowed from the wooden dock below. Offering Cathy a knowing nod, Sky descended the gangplank that had been dropped into position now they were docked.

'Bubus, my old friend. It has been too long since I visited Painted Point.'

Cathy watched from the ship as the two of them embraced. Knowing that Sky was able to transform into a dog made the exchange all the more curious. Cathy half expected cats and dogs to be of the same unfavourable nature in Mielikuvitus and yet here they were, embracing as long-lost friends.

'Why is it every time you come to my home, you come with a request of me and my people?'

'Cathy?' Sky shouted and turned to look at Cathy as she was eavesdropping on the deck above. 'Care to join in the conversation rather than listening to it?'

'It cannot be!' Bubus exclaimed, as he turned to look up at Cathy. 'Young Cathy Scott. How you've grown.'

'I'm sorry, have we met?'

Cathy walked down the gangplank, with Evie balancing on the wooden plank behind her. As far as she could remember, she had never seen Bubus or anyone like Flash when she had last visited Mielikuvitus. Somehow she liked to think she would have remembered a walking, talking cat.

'When you were but a baby in your mother's arms.'

Bubs stood a little shorter than Cathy and grabbed her, wrapping his pawed arms around her in a tight hug.

'I'm sorry, I don't remember.'

'Why would you?' Bubus laughed as he ruffled her hair and stepped away. 'Your mother and father visited with all of their children. I have seen you and both your brothers.'

'Why would they bring us here?'

'Because you are Partum and should always have a connection to Mielikuvitus.' Bubus read the confusion on Cathy's face and promptly changed his course of conversation. 'We should keep explanations for later. I would see you welcomed to Painted Point and see my town alive with celebrations that a Partum Spiritus once again walks among us.'

Without a chance to answer, the crowds were filled with chatter and excitement. Feeling her face blush, Cathy wanted to be away from the eyes that looked at her. Suddenly, even with Evie at her side, she felt self-conscious and out of place.

Hearing the way Bubs, and even Flash, spoke of her filled her with a feeling she wasn't what they expected. The confusion of the fight aboard the Lady Chance still haunted her, more so the fact she had felt no connection to the carved Aralcym Sky had given her.

Knowing that Timothy and Aiden had used their own weapons only left her feeling she didn't belong.

Deep down, Cathy questioned if the reason she had never been allowed to return to Mielikuvitus was because she wasn't supposed to. Flooded with embarrassment, she felt her eyes fill with tears and looked around for any hope of being alone.

'What's wrong?' Evie asked, seeing the tears in Cathy's eyes.

'I need a few minutes on my own.' She fought to hold back from crying, not out of fear but out of embarrassment and frustration.

Cathy's answer caught Evie by surprise, and before she could offer any form of comfort, Cathy sprinted back up to the deck of the Lady Chance. Hearing the crowds fall silent behind her, Cathy had no care for what they were thinking, she just needed to be alone. Arriving back on the deck she searched for the doors into the main hold and sprinted towards them.

'Is everything alright Cathy Scott?' Flash shouted after her as she slammed the doors shut behind her.

Stumbling on the bottom step, Cathy crashed to the damp deck and felt a sting of pain in her hand. Sitting up where she had fallen, Cathy checked her palm and saw a splinter of wood sticking out of her palm. Letting her tears fall, she ripped out the splinter and held her hand to her chest. Leaning back against the support beam of the main deck, she hugged her arms around her knees and wept.

'What's wrong, my dear?' Captain Flash asked as he peeked through the doors at the top of the staircase.

'I want to be alone.' Cathy snapped up at the captain.

'You should not be sad. My town is alive with excitement at you being here. Did you not hear them singing?'

'That's the problem.' Cathy sniffled as she wiped her face. 'You all seem to think I'm something I'm not.'

'And what would that be?' Flash crept to sit on the top step, not daring to approach any further.

'You all think I'm like Tim and Aiden or my mum and dad.'

'But you are.' Flash interrupted. 'You are like them, you are a Partum Spiritus.'

'No, I'm not.' Cathy's voice rose higher than she had intended and sensed Flash's shock. 'I was too small to be of much use when I was here last time and now, now I don't think I can do what they did.'

'But you have that.' Flash's paw pointed to the Aralcym at her side. 'Only a true Partum can wield such a weapon.'

'I know.' Cathy sighed, removing the Aralcym and holding it in her shaking hands. 'That's what I mean. I couldn't do anything with it when the Dark Queen attacked your ship.'

'Maybe you expect too much of yourself.' Flash soothed. 'Nobody can expect you to call the Eternal Flame without practice.'

'You all look at me like I should be able to.'

'That was not my intent.' Flash looked hurt as she watched him on the top step. 'If I have added to your worries, I offer my most sincere apologies. It was not my intention.'

'No, I didn't mean it like that.' Cathy's frustration bubbled over as she tossed the Aralcym to the floor. 'You see. I can't even get that right, you're trying to help and all I'm doing is making it worse for everyone.'

'I shall leave you to be alone as you desire.'

Before Cathy could argue, Flash removed himself from the staircase and disappeared back through the doors. Unable to hold back the tears, Cathy looked up towards the damp wooden ceiling and felt a wave of frustration wash over her. Closing her eyes, she felt the warm tears trail down her cheeks and allowed herself to listen only to the creaking of the ship and the gentle lapping of the sea against the smooth hull.

'I wish I could be home.' Cathy sighed to herself, the irony was not lost on her considering how long she had waited to come back through the mirror.

CHAPTER TEN

FITTING IN

'Enough wallowing.' Sky's voice declared, and Cathy opened her eyes.

Having been left alone in the sleeping quarters, it surprised her to see she was still alone. Wiping the sleep from her eyes, she scanned around and caught sight of Evie on the deck behind Sky.

'What time is it?'

'Early.' Sky snapped. His usual playfulness had evaporated. It reminded Cathy of the serious man she had met when Timothy had helped fight the Dark Entity. 'Gather yourself and join me on the deck, I would seek the chance to ease your worries.'

'I was...' Ignoring any protest, Sky stalked back through the door, leaving her alone.

Feeling sleep still clawing at her, Cathy shook her head and scooped up the Aralcym from the floor. Standing up, her head swam and vision danced with stars having moved too fast. Leaning against the beam by her side, she took a few long breaths before daring to move. A night's sleep on the damp wooden floor of the ship hadn't been her best idea. Her body now protested and ached in response.

Shaking away the sleepiness, she climbed the steep staircase and emerged back on the main deck. The night had been and gone and while there was a chill in the air; the sun had crept up above the horizon. The deck was shrouded in the shadow of the masts, and Cathy glanced up to see the crew fading from view as the sun's light touched their soft fur.

'Captain Flash told me of your conversation last night.'

Sky's voice caught Cathy by surprise and she turned to find him sat on a crossbeam above her. Craning her neck, she watched as he toyed with a length of rope that secured one of the sails in position. Tying the weathered rope in a complex knot, Sky was silent until he had finished and allowed the knotted rope to drop and hang in place.

'What did he tell you?' Cathy pressed, the silence making her feel uncomfortable.

'Nothing I hadn't already seen in your eyes.' Sky dropped from the crossbeam and landed on the deck in front of Cathy. 'Much like Timothy, you struggle to hide your emotions.'

'I don't know what you mean.' Cathy snapped.

'Exactly like that.' Sky offered a wry smile and ruffled Cathy's hair. 'You don't believe you are capable of the same things as your parents and brothers, do you?'

Once again feeling self-conscious, Cathy shook her head and dropped her gaze.

'You expect too much of yourself.' Evie added as she watched from the top deck. 'You shouldn't compare yourself to your brothers.'

'I'm almost as old as Tim was when he came here for the first time. I should be able to do what he could.'

'Evie is right.' Sky continued as he hung his brown cloak off the knotted rope. 'Timothy was no master when he first wielded his Nosym, I recall the battles he had calling forth the Eternal Flame.'

'I don't believe you.'

'Why don't I show you?'

The offer was well received, and for the rest of the day Sky and Cathy worked under the baking sun. Consumed by the concentration, and frustration, Cathy paid no attention to the faces that watched on from the dock below. As the afternoon bled away, Cathy had still not called even an ember from the open mouth of the dragon's stone face.

'I can't do it.' She bellowed in anger as she fought to catch her breath. 'I saw what you did against the Dark Queen and yet I can't manage anything.'

'Your mind is too heavy with expectation, you need to move through the fog you're creating.'

'That makes absolutely no sense.'

'That's enough for today.' Sky sighed as he struggled to hide his disappointment.

'No, I want to keep trying.'

'It would serve no purpose.' Sky explained as he slipped the fur-edged cloak over his shoulders. 'The more you fight with yourself, the further away your connection will be.'

'Show me.'

Cathy's voice overflowed with anger as she stamped her foot on the wooden deck and glared across at Sky. Meeting his gaze, she stared with anger into his canine eyes, but refused to back down or even blink.

Sky took a moment to decide. Cathy could see the elder weighing up his choices, his eyes moving from her to the movement of the ship and its invisible crew.

After a tense few moments, Sky fastened the cloak around his neck and moved to kneel in front of Cathy. Holding her chin, his expression softened enough to break Cathy's stubborn demands.

'My dear Cathy, I see so much confusion in you that I would not see you fall on your first attempt. Your brother was very much the same in the beginning. I promise you, it took him time to master his skills, you cannot expect so much in so little time.'

'How long will it take?'

'That, my dear, will be decided by you.'

'Then I want to do it now.'

Despite her posture, the childish demands gave away her youth. Hearing Cathy's tone, Sky could only smile as he released her chin and stood up.

'I cannot fault your tenacity, Cathy. Desire alone will not connect you with the Eternal Flame.' Cathy's shoulders dropped with disappointment. 'But there are things you can do, aside from practicing with your Aralcym.'

'Like what?'

'Come, I'll give you some homework while I show you around Painted Point.'

Cathy and Sky wandered along the twisting streets of the curious settlement, and Cathy drank in her surroundings as Sky spoke to her. She realised after a few moments that the houses and buildings were made of reclaimed ship parts and every so often Cathy could make out the outline of a hull or other familiar ship piece.

Moving deeper into the town, Cathy caught glimpses of the sea between the slats of wood that made up the surface of the streets. She had never imagined having found an entirely floating city made of reclaimed ships and yet, here she was, once again surrounded by the impossible.

Sky guided Cathy past the various shops and stalls and into the residential centre of the floating town. Quickly the air was filled with the glorious smell of food cooking, and before long, Cathy could almost hear her stomach rumbling over the gentle breeze that whistled around the rooftops.

'I do believe your experiences in Mielikuvitus may be a reason for you struggling to find a connection.' Sky began as they moved towards an impressive house that dominated the area ahead of them.

'What do you mean?'

'You were too young to have crossed when you did.' Sky confessed as he guided Cathy towards the oversized structure. 'Your connection to our world came through your kidnapper, not through an Ecilop as is our tradition.'

'You mean Minnie?'

'I still struggle to understand the reasons for your connection, but yes, Minnie.'

'Tim had his Ecilop for as long as he could remember but Aiden didn't get his until he came through to rescue me.'

'Every Partum's time is different.' Sky exhaled. 'Your mother was but a young girl when she realised her connection. Your father and Aiden were a little older.'

'Will I have an Ecilop?'

'That is not your path.' Sky explained as footsteps behind the door grew louder. 'Your connection to Minnie was your first relationship with our world. Evie was sent to be your lifelong companion, bridging our worlds.'

Cathy realised Evie had been padding in silence behind them, as they had navigated the town. Offering her friend a smile, Cathy couldn't help but laugh as Evie offered her a cheeky wink.

'Think of your connection like a fledgling bird,' Sky explained as the locks behind the door were unlocked. 'You form a bond with the first creature of Mielikuvitus. Yours was Minnie, a beast of our world.'

'So why Evie once Minnie was...dead? Why not an Ecilop?'

'Thanks.' Evie barked, and Cathy was quick to apologise.

'I didn't mean it like that, and you know it.'

'Evie is very much akin to Minnie. The Hecate are nomadic creatures, born to wander the lands as they see fit. Much like Minnie, Evie here remains one of the few remaining of her kind.'

'Is that what connects us, being isolated?'

'Oh my dear girl, you're not alone. You have a loving family with you.'

'I don't feel the same as them. I'm always left feeling they have their stories of battles and war, while I will always just be their little girl.'

'You simply haven't discovered your path yet, it makes you no lesser than any of them.' Sky's words offered a little comfort as the door was pulled open.

Grateful for the distraction, Sky turned his attention to the now open door and Bubus-anjam who was standing in the shadowed entry.

'A late greeting is better than no greeting at all.' Bubus beamed at Cathy, his crooked whiskers twitching.

'I'm sorry, I didn't mean to be rude last night.'

'Behave young Cathy Scott.' Bubus roared with laughter. 'I am blessed to stand in the presence of a Partum Spiritus, never mind having to wait a little longer for the honour.'

'I'm not...'

'We are honoured to be welcomed into your town and your home, Bubus.' Sky interrupted Cathy before she could finish her apology.

'Come inside, my family are waiting.'

Ushered in through the door, it amazed Cathy to find the interior of the house decorated in bright floral patterns and colours. The inside looked like nothing she had expected and, for a moment, she felt like she had wandered into some elderly relative's home. It reminded her of her great-aunt, an extravagant woman who smelled of too much perfume and had a rather unhealthy fondness for flowery patterns and lace.

Grateful for the distraction, Cathy followed Bubus deeper into the house to meet his family.

'These are my daughters, Mira and Mew.'

Two juvenile felines sauntered into the room and stopped in the doorway. Judging by their size, Cathy guessed them to be a year or two younger than her. Offering the two girls a smile, Bubus guided Cathy to a large table filled with steaming bowls of food.

'Nice to meet you all.' Cathy offered with a broad smile.

'I'm sad that you will not get the chance to meet my wife.' The smile on Bubus' face waned a little. 'She passed away during the winter.'

'I'm sorry to hear that.' Sky's voice was filled with sadness. 'I will always remember her warm smile and hospitality.'

'And her Sea Swirl Soup.' Bubus pushed aside the sadness and allowed his smile to return. 'I must confess, my daughters and I have never made it the way she did, but I hope you'll agree that it's not the worst you have tasted.'

Mira and Mew flanked Cathy on either side as Sky sat opposite beside Bubus. Grateful for the food, unsure of what she was eating, Cathy wolfed down the deep pot of steaming soup. It was hard to describe what the Sea Swirl tasted of, but as she finished her first bowl, Cathy was eager to accept the offer of a second portion.

The evening rolled by with shared stories and laughter. It was not long before Cathy had cast aside the disappointment at her inability to call the Eternal Flame. As Bubus and Sky sat in hushed conversation; she found amusement with Evie and the girls.

CHAPTER ELEVEN

ORANGE SMOKE

Cathy spent the next week splitting her time between Bubus' daughters and Sky's teaching. Still she could not feel any sort of connection with the Aralcym, but Sky had changed his tact and focussed on finding a way to repair the damage and lingering doubt Cathy carried with her.

As the morning broke on their eighth day at Painted Point, Sky had Cathy poised on the tallest of the crossbeams on the mainmast of the Lady Chance. It had taken all of her courage to climb to the top of the mast and Cathy had spent more than a good length of time gripping the ropes and hugging the mast while Sky balanced on the crossbeam.

'I can feel the ship moving with the waves.' Cathy's voice trembled as she looked down at the deck far below.

Trying not to look down only exacerbated her worries, as Cathy could see the gentle sway of the ship as the waves lapped against the hull. With her fingers white, she gripped the mast and threw a furious glare at Sky on the crossbeam below.

'It doesn't seem so bad to me.' Sky laughed as he tiptoed along the length of the wooden beam.

Sky looked at ease with the height and kept secure footing as he moved. Cathy could see he was timing each step with the rocking of the ship, but it wasn't something she felt comfortable doing.

'You're joking if you think I'm going to let go.' Cathy cursed as she stared at the lengths of rope wrapped around the mainmast. 'There's nothing to stop me if I fall down.'

'I'll catch you.' Sky offered, but Cathy was not convinced.

'Not a chance.'

'You need to let go of some of your fears. They hold you back where you should flourish and fly.'

'Fly? You talk about flying now? Right now?'

The fact Sky laughed at Cathy's terrified reply didn't help. Still hugging the wooden mast, Cathy longed to get down but was too afraid to even let go to reach for the hanging rope ladder she had climbed up.

'A poor choice of words, I know. Sorry.' Sky stifled his laughter as he looked up at Cathy.

'That's not helping.'

'What?'

'Laughing at me!'

Despite everything, Cathy couldn't help but allow the corners of her mouth to lift as she tried to hide her own amusement. Sensing Sky's knowing expression, she forced herself to release one hand from the wooden mast.

'Good.' Sky coaxed as he watched Cathy's shaking hand stretch out in front of her. 'Just take a single step, let yourself be free of your fears.'

The mention of fear sent Cathy recoiling back to the safety of the wood. Wrapping her arms around it again, she fought to settle her ragged breaths and felt her own frustration rising. Not wanting to fail again, she steeled herself for another try.

Moving with great care, she let go with one hand and shuffled her feet a little further from the mast. Feeling the gentle breeze at her back, she tried to press her feet harder into the crossbeam. Feeling her knees shaking, Cathy ignored Sky and focussed her attention on the cliffs and beach far behind Painted Point.

'Everything will be fine.' The sound of Evie's voice in her head was nearly enough to undo her balance. 'I'm here with you.'

Looking down and instantly regretting it, Cathy caught sight of Evie sat looking up from the deck below. Not wanting to let her friend down, Cathy swallowed hard and shuffled her feet even further along the crossbeam.

Cathy moved along until her hand only gripped a tether of coiled rope wrapped around the mast. Counting in her head, she willed her fingers to loosen and let go of their vice-like grip on the rope. Taking a deep breath, tasting the salty sea air, she closed her eyes and released her fingers.

Wobbling in position, Cathy kept her eyes clamped shut as she fought to calm her racing heart. Hearing the waves over the thumping in her ears, Cathy slowly opened her eyes and could no longer hide the broad grin that painted across her face.

'I'm doing it!' She shrieked and looked down at Sky.

Cathy would never have believed she could have done it. She had been hugging the mast for what felt like the entire day and yet now she was standing on the crossbeam keeping her own balance. Wobbling as she fought to remain balanced, Cathy saw the look on Sky's face and swelled with pride.

What happened next was over in a heartbeat, but for Cathy, it felt like an age. Without warning, a loud bugle blurted from the docks. The sound startled Cathy and instantly her concentration lapsed. As the musical fanfare subsided, Cathy fought to keep her balance on the rocking crossbeam.

She had moved too far to launch herself back towards the mast. Rocking back and forth, she thrust out her arms like a circus-performer to keep herself balanced. It was a pointless gesture. Her arms did nothing to stabilise her precarious perch, and Cathy felt herself overbalance forward.

With nothing to grab hold of, Cathy slipped from the crossbeam and tumbled down towards the deck. It almost felt as if she was seeing the world in slow motion as the folded sails whipped in front of her face. Feeling the pull of gravity, Cathy closed her eyes and screamed.

Cathy was sure her descent was slower than it should have been. Somehow she expected to have crashed into the wooden deck by now, but hadn't. In fact, as she thought about it, the wind no longer whipped past her face and she felt like she wasn't moving.

Daring to open her eyes, Cathy was almost sick, as she now saw the deck above her head and the sky at her feet. Suspended in midair, Cathy had fallen about half the distance between the highest crossbeam and the ground below.

'How?' Was all she could muster as her dress threatened to fall over her head at any moment.

'I told you.' Sky heaved. 'I would have you if you fell.'

Feeling herself moving through the air, Cathy reached out and took hold of the rope ladder in front of her. Feeling whatever magic had taken hold of her released, gravity took control and she fell to land the right way up, gripping the rope rung. Gasping for breath, Cathy entwined her hands through the ladder and held on for dear life.

'How did you do that?' Cathy huffed as she made her way back down to the deck.

'I have spent many years devoted to the ways of all creatures of Mielikuvitus. In my studies, I have mastered but a handful of skills that seek to aid my role as mentor and guide.'

'So, you can use magic?'

'No, not at all. I am simply in tune, on a very basic level, with the elements of Mielikuvitus. It allows me to make the slightest of manipulations, as I did just then.'

Cathy was grateful to feel the solid deck beneath her feet and looked up to see Sky descending the ladder not far above. Moving to the side, she wrapped her fingers in Evie's silky coat as she sauntered over to join her.

'You look tired.' Evie remarked as Sky dropped to the deck and wiped the sweat from his brow.

'Much like when I used your Aralcym, I am not a creature that is supposed to wield these powers. Whereas it comes as second nature to those who should, it requires a lot of effort from me to master even the simplest of tasks.'

'It's not second nature to me.' Cathy scoffed but fell silent with the stern gaze Sky threw her.

'Bubus announced arrivals.' Evie added, breaking the tension between Cathy and Sky.

'We are not expecting company.' Sky mused as he looked towards Painted Point and a plume of orange smoke that billowed into the air. 'It was not an announcement of battle but the smokes warn of danger.'

'Smokes?'

'Come, we should meet with Bubus and find out why the smoke has been lit.'

Falling into place beside Sky, Cathy struggled to keep pace as they raced from the Lady Chance towards Bubus' curious home. Navigating the streets was easier now that Cathy was familiar with the town, but it was easy to get turned about amongst the collection of buildings and structures. Losing sight of Sky ahead of her, Cathy took a path that found her facing a dead-end road in the centre of the town.

'Sky?' She pressed as the sounds of chattering crowds carried from the streets behind her.

Looking around at the array of shops down the narrow alleyway, Cathy found her attention drawn to a dusty window looking out onto the alley. Moving closer, something behind the obscured glass caught her attention, catching the slithers of light that broke through the layers of dust and cobwebs.

Placing her hand against the glass, Cathy brushed aside the dust and stared at a strange mask displayed in an ornate glass case. The mask was simple in its design, painted white with a dark blue pattern etched on the front. Where the eyeholes should be were two orbs of shimmering blue glass that glinted in the sunlight.

'Help you?' A gruff voice barked from the doorway to her side.

'Sorry?'

Cathy turned to look at the source of the voice and recoiled in surprise. Feeling her heart skip a beat, the creature that had spoken to her was a Croinsop. Backing away, Cathy fumbled at her side to grab the Aralcym handle as her back crashed into the solid wall at the end of the narrow road.

'Calm yourself.' The Croinsop snarled. 'I mean you no harm.'

'Stay away from me.' Cathy hissed as she gripped the Aralcym, 'I know what you are.'

The Croinsop paused for a moment and offered Cathy a curious look.

'I hold no love for my ancestors.' The Croinsop spat a mouthful of yellow bile onto the floor at his feet. 'I am an outcast of my people and better off for it. I offer you no ill will.'

'I need to go.'

'You'll not find me blocking your path.' The Croinsop offered and moved aside. 'You'll do well to follow back to the road and take a right.'

'Thank you.' Cathy offered as she moved warily past the Croinsop.

'You're welcome.' He replied, his pincers clicking together as he spoke. 'Cathy Scott.'

Cathy didn't hear her name spoken as she jogged back to the main thoroughfare, seeking to put as much distance as she could between her and the creature that haunted her nightmares.

CHAPTER TWELVE

GONKS VENIT

As Cathy found her way back to the square outside Bubus' curious house, she stopped dead in her tracks. The sight that met her was something she had never expected as the air was filled with music and two rows of chickens marched down the street towards Bubus.

Mouth wide, Cathy couldn't believe what she was seeing. As the eight chickens marched in unison, they looked completely normal, except for the muscular arms that protruded from their chests. Sticking out from between the feathers were human hands, veiny and muscular, that looked completely at odds with their feathery bodies.

Trying not to laugh, Cathy watched the precession march in time towards Bubus who remained on his raised doorstep. When they reached the threshold the lead chicken, a grey feathered hen, clucked and raised her right hand into the air, bringing the troop to a stop.

Hearing their long claws clicking on the wooden floor, the eight of them snapped to attention and waved their arms in the air. Perfectly in time they wobbled their fluffy backsides, squatted and pooped on the floor.

'Welcome, friends.' Bubus beamed, and the chickens lowered their arms, letting them once again hand in front of their puffy chests.

The grey chicken that had brought the troop to a halt now shook her head, her red comb wobbling from side-to-side as she ruffled her feathers.

'Captain Bubus-Anjam, we the Chigems seek your help.'

'How might we help the honoured explorers of the underground?'

'The armies of the Dark Queen have invaded our homes and hold the Chigem Mines hostage.'

The atmosphere in the square fell silent, and all gathered eyes directed towards the quivering chicken. Despite their almost comical appearance, Cathy could feel the fear and tension in the air at the mention of the Dark Queen.

'Cathy.' Bubus declared. 'Come, join me and the Chigems.'

Emerging from the crowd of gathered habitants of Painted Point, Cathy stepped forward and past the two rows of chickens. Doing her best not to stare at their oversized and out of proportion arms, Cathy moved to join Bubus.

'What's going on?' Cathy asked, taking in the look of concern on Bubus' face.

'We should speak inside.' Bubus mused. 'Too many faces and ears for a conversation that I fear, may give us grave concern.'

Without a word, Bubus turned and walked through the house. Before Cathy could follow, the eight Chigems filed through the door, brushing past her legs as they went. Following behind the troop, the door closed behind Cathy as she moved back through Bubus' home and into the familiar dining room.

'Clarice, Everest, Daisy, Hetty, Jade, Ethal, Elsa and Rex. I am honoured to welcome you into my home.' Bubus welcomed the individual Chigems into the dining room. 'I only wish it were under better circumstances.'

Cathy watched as the eight chickens hopped up onto the long dining table and waited for Bubus to take his seat. Feeling out of place, Cathy edged towards the table and waited to be welcomed to the curious meeting.

Everything about this felt and looked ridiculous. Not only were the chickens talking, but their oversized arms added to the strangeness of what was happening. Cathy caught Bubus' gaze, and he welcomed her to the table with a subtle nod.

'Who is this?' The grey Chigem asked as Cathy took her seat.

'This is Cathy Scott, daughter of Susan and Gerard.' Bubus announced with great pride. 'She is a Partum Spiritus.'

Cathy blushed as eight pairs of beady eyes turned to look at her. The lead Chigem pushed past the others and moved to stand on the table in front of Cathy. Frozen in place, Cathy tried her hardest not to laugh as the Chigem's muscular arms bobbed up and down with each step.

Reaching her, the Chigem craned her neck and tilted her head to one side while staring at Cathy. Feeling the beady eyes boring into her, Cathy held her breath while the curious creature tapped her beak against Cathy's nose and cheeks.

'What are you doing?' Cathy hushed as the Chigem tapped her bottom lip.

'Tasting your aura.' The Chigem declared. 'You are indeed a child of our lands. How did you come to be here?'

'That's a long story.' Bubus answered on Cathy's behalf. 'But, Clarice, now is not the time for Cathy's story. I am eager to hear yours.'

Clarice remained in front of Cathy for a few more seconds before turning her attention back to Bubus. Sitting back, Cathy listened as the Chigems explained the course of events that had led them to escape the armies of the Dark Queen.

'They arrived in the middle of the night.' Clarice began, her words heavy with regret. 'We were powerless to resist and the Dark Queen's troll army overran the mines in a matter of minutes. They killed many hundreds of our sisters as we tried our best to fight them back.'

'It did not take them long to destroy our defences.' Rex, one of the brown-feathered Chigems, continued. 'With nothing left to hold them back, the Dark Queen arrived and offered us a choice.'

'What choice did she give you?' Cathy pressed.

'To save those of us who had not fallen, we would have to return to the mines in search of treasures of old.'

'They are a myth.' Sky interrupted, his voice stern as he stepped into the room. 'Nothing more than a bedtime story.'

'Story or not, the Dark Queen decimated our home and imprisoned us.' Clarice snapped. 'And until we can give her what she wants, there will be no freedom from her dark clutches.'

'What was she looking for?'

'We cannot sit back while the Chigems are held captive.' Bubus continued, ignoring Cathy's question.

'We come in search of help.' Clarice continued.

'What is she looking for?' Cathy asked again.

'The Dark Queen seems intent on destroying everything in search of fairy tales.' Sky sighed as he moved to Bubus' side.

'What is she looking for?'

'Regardless of her reasons, we cannot sit idly by and leave them to suffer.'

'WHAT IS SHE LOOKING FOR?' Cathy's voice echoed around the dining room as everyone fell silent and turned to look at her.

'Fairy tales.' Sky sighed.

'Don't treat me like a child.' Cathy warned, rising from her seat and placing her hands on the tabletop. 'You keep telling me to trust my instincts and pushing me to accept what I am. So tell me what she's looking for.'

'If what Clarice says is true.' Sky took a long breath. 'The Dark Queen is searching for the Gonks-Venit stones.'

'And what exactly are they?'

'Eight mythical stones, birthed from the bedrock of Mielikuvitus and enriched with the power of the Eternal Flame.' As Clarice spoke, her voice was filled with wonder and awe. 'The Chigems have long believed they would find the stones. It was the reason we settled at the foot of the Golden Slopes hundreds of years ago.'

'They aren't real.' Sky protested.

'Then why does your hand shake?' Rex retorted, and Cathy turned her attention to Sky.

The Chigem was not wrong. Sky looked more uncomfortable than she had ever seen, and the fact he could not hold her gaze told her Sky was lying. Holding his gaze, Cathy waited for Sky to explain what was happening.

'You really are just like Timothy.' Sky groaned and moved to take a sit next to Bubus.

All eyes turned to Sky as he rested his elbow on the table and toyed with his greying beard. The room was uncomfortably silent as Sky mused over his answer. After what felt like an age, Sky lifted his head and directed his answer to the gathered faces around the large table.

'Legend speaks of a time when Mielikuvitus was still taking shape. As the lands formed and mountains grew towards the sky, our worlds were entwined.' Sky raised his hands and Cathy gasped as a layer of smoke lifted from the table's surface. 'At first, the portals between our worlds were uncontrolled. You could easily step between the barriers and find yourself on one side or the other. It was not until the worlds had forged their connection that our worlds separated and there were but tendrils left.'

'Like the mirror at home?'

'Just like the mirror, Cathy, yes.' Sky smiled as the smoke on the table took shape and played out the explanation Sky was giving.

'There remains just a handful of connections between your home and ours. The Gonks-Venit are said to exist to collapse the divide and once again draw our worlds together and fuse as a single place.'

'How would that work?' Cathy pressed. 'Surely it can't work, otherwise there would be no need for two separate worlds.'

'True.' The smoke took the form of two planets side-by side. 'For both our worlds to exist in parallel keeps the balance, should the divide be fully bridged it would not be possible for both to survive in isolation.'

'What would happen?'

Sky manipulated the smoky orbs, and all eyes watched as the two worlds collided and fought to consume one another. The atmosphere was tense as the two worlds fought and struggled to dominate over the other until the smoke exploded. Cathy shielded her eyes from the sudden burst of smoke and as she uncovered them she faced a shape she did not recognise. It was no longer a smooth orb. Instead it was jagged, uneven and oddly unnerving.

'If our worlds combine, neither will survive.' Sky's words were laced with dismay. 'What would remain would be nothing more than darkness and destruction. A new world that would see us all destroyed.'

'Why would the Dark Queen want that?'

'It would be a new world, created by her hand, that she could rule and forge in her own image.'

'But they're not real? You said so, right?'

Once again, Sky looked uncomfortable.

'I have lived my life in the hope the Gonks-Venit were nothing more than a myth.' Sky allowed the apparition to disappear. 'The Dark Queen's actions tell me she believes they are real.'

'Is that why she brought me here?'

'I believe it so.' Sky rose from his seat and moved back to the open door. 'Bubus is right, we cannot leave the Chigems to suffer at the hand of the Dark Queen.'

'What are we going to do?' Cathy asked as Sky moved to leave.

'We?' Sky sighed. 'We will do nothing. Bubus will afford me Captain Flash and as many ships as he can spare to free the Chigems.'

'What about me?'

'You will stay here with Bubus.'

'No, I want to help.'

'Cathy!' Sky barked, his voice rumbling. 'The Dark Queen would relish another chance to take you and without knowing the Gonks-Venit remain hidden beneath the ground, I cannot risk you being taken by her again.'

'That's not fair.' Cathy stamped her feet in defiance.

'This is not up for debate.' Sky snapped. 'Bubus will oversee your training in my absence.'

'I will call the fleet, we will have a dozen ships by daybreak.'

'Thank you.'

Not giving Cathy a chance to argue, Sky stalked out of the room, leaving Cathy, Bubus and the eight Chigems behind him in stunned silence. Cathy could feel all eyes on her and longed to be alone. Once again she felt like she was nothing more than a hindrance to everything she touched, more pain than help.

Stifling her tears, she excused herself and all but sprinted out of the dining room.

Chapter Thirteen

Armada

Painted Point became a hive of activity throughout the evening and into the night. Having found herself a hiding place, in a small dwelling near to where she had encountered the Croinsop, Cathy listened to the hustle and bustle.

Voices filled the air and as night descended she saw the Thunders appear as the sunlight no longer hid them from view. Everyone moved with haste, making preparations for the ships that Bubus had recalled the docks.

'I've been looking for you everywhere.' Evie's now familiar voice scorned as her pale-furred companion padded along the alley to join her.

'I needed to be alone.'

'Even from me?' There was genuine hurt in Evie's voice.

'Even you.'

'Do you want me to leave go?' Evie paused in the alleyway's mouth and waited for Cathy's answer.

'No, I don't want you to go.'

With Evie curled around her feet, Cathy felt comfort and ruffled her companion's head to keep herself distracted. Coiling her fur between her fingers, Cathy spoke to Evie as they sat alone in the alley.

'Why won't Sky let me go?'

'I'm sure he has his reasons.' Evie answered as she nuzzled Cathy's hand. 'He's only looking out for you.'

'It's because I'm not Tim.' Cathy huffed. 'It's because no matter how hard I try, I can't do anything he can.'

'You'll get there Cathy. It will just take time.'

'But I want to help. Being left behind isn't going to help me, is it?'

'If Sky thinks it's right.'

'If he's the only one that can train me, the whole time he's gone I'll be getting nowhere.'

Evie knew Cathy well enough and moved to sit in front of her. With Cathy hunched against the wall, Evie was almost nose-to-nose with Cathy as she looked at her.

'You're not thinking of going, are you?'

'You know me so well, Eevs!' Cathy could not hide the wry smile on her face.

'I don't think it's a good idea. Not at all.'

'I won't sit by and do nothing. If Sky thinks I'm capable of doing what Tim and Aiden did, then he has to carry on training me.'

'I'm not sure about this.'

'I won't force you to come with me, but I've decided.'

'I won't leave your side.'

'That's settled then.'

Despite Evie's protests, Cathy emerged from the alley and made her way to the docks. All but ignored by the crowds of creatures, they made good time to the dock and soon found themselves looking up at the vast array of ships that had joined the Lady Chance.

'How many are there?' Cathy gasped as she did her best to count the dozens of ships that sat anchored a little away from the docks. 'How did they get so many in such a short amount of time?'

'Bubus has many at his beck and call. The Lady Chance is the pride of the Thunderan fleet and Captain Flash, his best sailor.'

The sound of Sky's voice carried in the air, and Cathy scanned the crowds of people milling around the dock. Catching sight of her mentor, she saw the same troubled look on his face and knew she was best staying out of sight.

Looking around, Cathy saw a large collection of crates and boxes being hoisted into the air and made a run for it. With Evie hot on her tail, Cathy sprinted through the crowd and jumped onto the slowly lifting crate just in time. Hiding herself amongst the boxes, she made enough space for her and Evie and waited.

As they hoisted the cargo into the air, it reminded Cathy of the hours she had spent balancing on the crossbeams of the Lady Chance's sails. She could say one thing as she listened to the creaking ropes. She was no longer afraid of heights. Peering down between the slats of the floor, she scanned the crowds and caught sight of Sky.

Sky was deep in conversation, but nobody stood by his side. As the cargo passed in front of the sun, its shadow cast over Sky, and she caught a fleeting glimpse of Captain Flash by Sky's side. Flash was dressed in a new waistcoat and sported a green and black bandana over the top of his head. Smiling, Cathy saw he had cut two holes to allow his feline ears to protrude through the fabric.

As they lifted Cathy over the Lady Chance, she watched as Flash pointed up towards her hiding place and for a split second thought that Flash had seen her. Holding her breath, despite it making no difference, Cathy watched with bated breath as Flash peered up towards her and winked.

Knowing she had been seen, her heart raced in her chest but as the crate moved and the sun forced Flash to disappear again, she waited to see if he had betrayed her to Sky. Peering through the crates as she was lowered into the cargo hold, Cathy breathed a sigh of relief as Sky was directed away from the Lady Chance and her secret hiding place.

'That was close.' Cathy sighed as the pallet of boxes was dropped to the deck.

'I don't like this.' Evie complained as Cathy slipped from between the boxes.

'I know, you keep saying.' Cathy scoffed as she looked around at the cargo hold. 'I have said you can stay behind.'

'And you know my answer to that!'

Evie pushed past Cathy as the pair searched for somewhere to hide amongst the scattered cargo. Although the hold was fairly full, Cathy suspected the crew would work busily through the night to secure as much as they could for the voyage ahead. As she crossed the breadth of the cargo hold, a sudden noise stopped her in her tracks.

The sound was all too familiar and chilled her to the core. Scanning the dark space, she caught sight of a familiar silhouette as the Croinsop from the alleyway stepped into view. Her natural reaction was to scream, but Cathy knew that would bring the crew of the Lady

Chance running and ruin her chances to stowaway on the ship.

Sensing the change in Cathy, Evie snarled as she moved to her side. Baring her razor-sharp teeth, the Croinsop stopped in its tracks and lifted a flickering lantern up to its head height. Passing the lantern from its hand to the crooked pincer above its head, the Croinsop removed a pipe from beneath its shell and lit it.

'Strange place to see you again, Miss Scott.'

Cathy shivered as the Croinsop pronounced her name. Illuminated by the flickering flame, Cathy couldn't help but stare at the hard scorpion shell and for the first time realised the Croinsop was without a tail or stinger. The more she looked at the creature's skin and shell, the more battered and broken it appeared. At least one of its legs had been broken and hung limp, while both pincers looked like they had seen better days. A sinister-looking scar stretched down the entire right side of its face as it drew in the smoke from the wooden pipe.

'How do you know my name?'

'Everybody in Painted Point has whispered your name since you arrived.' The Croinsop muttered as it moved to perch on a barrel. 'When I laid eyes on you outside my shop, I thought it too good to be true.'

Acting on instinct, Cathy wrapped her hand around the bound handle of the Aralcym. Sensing the movement the Croinsop raised both hands into the air while pinning the pipe in the corner of its mouth.

'Rest easy, Miss Scott. I mean you no harm.'

'The last time I met your kind, you were ready to kill my family.'

'Quite right you are.' The Croinsop chuckled as it puffed out a lungful of sour-smelling smoke. 'The actions of my disgusting kind are not easily forgotten.'

The declaration caught Cathy by surprise, and while she lowered her guard, Evie remained at her side with teeth bared.

'Aren't you one of them?' Cathy's curiosity had been piqued.

'I was a soldier once, yes.' There was a tinge of regret in its voice. 'The greatest dishonour for my kind is for our tails to be removed, a sign that we are weak to defend ourselves.'

'Why would they do that to you?'

'Because I refused to follow the call of the darkness and whispers left by the Dark Entity.' The Croinsop puffed on the pipe for a moment before continuing. 'I turned my back and was banished from that moment.'

'How did you end up here, at Painted Point?'

'As a wary traveller in search of a home. Alas, Bubus-Anjam listened to my pleas and offered me sanctuary here in return for my trade.'

'You're a trader?'

'So many questions.' He laughed. 'Indeed, the stock of the ships are supplied from my warehouses. This sudden turn of events is most advantageous for my business.'

'I'll bet it is.' Evie snarled.

'Easy, Hecate. I offer no ill will to you or your master.'

'I'm not her master.' Cathy corrected. 'She's my friend.'

'My apologies, your customs are strange to me but I meant no offence.'

A voice carried from the deck and the Croinsop stiffened. Hearing his name bellowed from above, he ripped the pipe from his mouth and spilled the smouldering contents on the floor before stamping them out.

'Quick, I would not see you discovered amongst my wares.'

Beckoning to her, Cathy jumped as the doors to the upper deck opened and the sunlight streamed into the cargo hold. With little choice, Cathy and Evie dived into the shadows as the Croinsop moved a handful of boxes into position to hide them from view.

'Wonereheb, are you down there?' It was Sky's voice that carried down the steps.

The Croinsop leant over the barrels and thrust something wrapped in fabric into Cathy's hands. It had some weight to it, and Cathy was unsure what the Croinsop was doing. Before she could say anything, she heard Sky's footsteps descending the stairs and pressed herself back into the shadows.

'A small gift, Miss Scott, an apology for the pain my kind has caused you in the past. It is not much, but it is a token of my kindness to you.'

Lifting another box into position, Cathy lost all view of the cargo hold as she saw Sky approaching from behind the Croinsop.

'What keeps you so long?' She heard Sky press from the other side of the boxes.

'I found myself distracted for a moment.'

Cathy held her breath again, waiting for the Croinsop to betray her.

'Distracted with what?'

'Something very special.' Cathy peeked through a narrow gap and recoiled when she saw how close Sky was to her.

'It must have been to keep you from making even more money.' It was clear in Sky's tone he was no fan of the business-creature. 'Another ship has arrived in port and I would see her supplied and ready to sail at dawn.'

'I shall set to the task at once.'

As the two of them left the cargo hold, Cathy once again relaxed and sat back with the wrapped item on her lap. With enough space for her and Evie in the hideaway, it overcame Cathy with curiosity as she unwrapped the parcel.

Pulling the fabric aside, she gasped as the face of the curious mask she had seen through the window looked up at her. Feeling the smooth white mask with her finger, there were no features to it. The two eyeholes were covered in a shimmering translucent lens while black lines had been painted down the face. Admiring the mask, Cathy turned it over and was surprised to see words etched into the underside of the mask in a language she did not recognise.

'That's amazing.' Evie gasped as she moved closer to admire the mask.

'What is it?'

'That's a warrior mask. They're no longer used and most are kept as show pieces. That's precious.'

'Why would he give it to me?'

'I have no idea.' Evie answered as she curled herself up on the floor. 'Maybe we should get some sleep. I expect we'll be sailing as soon as the ships are ready.

CHAPTER FOURTEEN

SETTING SAIL

The armada of ships set sail as the dawn broke and it wasn't long before Painted Point had disappeared from sight. Concealed within the hold, Cathy had broken into the crates and soon found a stash of food to keep her from having to venture up deck to find something to eat.

With no view outside, Cathy missed the majestic landscapes as the ships turned into the mouth of Rainbow River and began their journey inland. Feeling only the rocking motion of the enormous ship, Cathy soon felt her stomach churning as she sat hugging her knees.

'You're looking green.' Evie nuzzled against Cathy and sniffed her ears. 'You need some fresh air.'

'I can hardly go up on deck, if they find me they'll go mad.'

Cathy felt a lump form in her throat as she fought to hold down the feeling of sick that was bubbling up from her stomach. Hugging her knees tight, she closed her eyes and tried to concentrate on something other than the motion of the ship. Hearing the waves lapping against the hull made that almost impossible, and before long, Cathy needed to release the contents of her stomach.

'I'm going to be sick!' Cathy exclaimed and slapped her hand over her mouth.

Launching from her hiding place, Cathy sprinted across the hold and up the stairs to the deck.

'Cathy, don't!' But it was too late.

Cathy burst onto the deck and crashed into one of the invisible crew. Ignoring the shouts and protests, Cathy made it to the railing as she was violently sick over the side of the ship. Staring down at the crystal blue water, Cathy caught her breath as she waited to see if she was going to be sick again.

'What is this?' Sky's familiar voice bellowed from somewhere behind her, but she dared not turn around to look.

'Sky, let me explain.' Evie protested as she padded to Cathy's side.

Being sick again, Cathy felt the burning in her mouth and knew there was nothing left in her stomach. Wiping her mouth with the back of her hand, she turned around to see Sky storming towards her.

The look on his face was easy to read. Brow furrowed and eyes narrowed, Sky was beyond angry as he towered over Cathy and glared down at her.

'What are you doing here?' His voice betrayed his canine nature as he all but growled the question.

'Give me a minute, I don't feel great.'

'Cathy Scott.' Sky snapped, catching Cathy by surprise. 'Explain yourself.'

Cathy felt her cheeks flush as Sky fought to contain his anger, but she had known this would happen at some point, just not as quick as it had. Steeling her resolve, she moved past Sky and took a deep breath to compose herself before offering him her answer.

'I wasn't going to sit there and wait like a spare part while you were gone for who knows how long?'

'It was not your choice to make.'

'Yes, it was.' Cathy kept her voice level, knowing she was treading on thin ice with Sky. 'I'm already struggling to get a control over this stupid thing, how was I supposed to protect myself if you were gone for days, weeks or even longer?'

'Bubus had agreed to keep up your training.'

'Can he teach me the way you can?'

It was Sky's turn to be caught off-guard. Cathy had prepared her argument, and despite his anger, Sky couldn't help but admire her tenacity.

'No, he can't.'

'Then what use would it be? I can learn things at school, but you need to show me. I'm never going to get control of it if you don't show me.'

Having practiced this speech over and over in her head, Cathy snatched the Aralcym from her side and held it in her quivering hand. There was an innocence in her face, almost pleading as she held the weapon in her hand.

'You're not ready.' Sky sighed and placed his hand on top of hers, his expression softening. 'All I wanted to do was to protect you.'

'But I want to protect myself.' Cathy struggled to hide the tears welling in her eyes. 'Will I ever be ready?'

Sky dropped to his knees and held Cathy's gaze. He could see the fire burning behind the tears in her eyes and knew the passion was inside her. Despite everything he had done with her, she had not found her connection to the Eternal Flame, and he saw how much it frustrated her. Taking a moment, Sky stared into Cathy's eyes, as if searching for an ember somewhere deep inside her.

'You are your mother's daughter.' Sky's voice was softer. 'The same fire burns in you as does in her. You will find your connection. Come, follow me.'

Without another word, Sky led Cathy up to the top deck and past the ship's wheel.

'Nice to see you aboard again, Cathy.' Flash's voice hushed as she moved past the invisible ship's captain.

'Thank you.'

Moving to the back of the ship, it afforded Cathy a view of Mielikuvitus and the lapping waters of Rainbow River. Sailing through the water behind them were a dozen ships, smaller than the Lady Chance but nonetheless an impressive sight to behold. Drinking in the array of coloured sails, Cathy scanned each of the ships and then moved her attention to the landscape that surrounded her.

In the distance she could see the snowy peaks of the Torn Mountains and felt a sudden sadness fill her heart. Not wanting to dwell on the sad memory of Minnie, Cathy moved her gaze from the mountains and looked further ahead of the ship.

'What's that?' Cathy asked as she settled her gaze on the array of enormous trees that lined the banks.

'That is Spine Forest.' Sky explained as he pointed out to the oversized trees. 'Behind that lies the gem caverns, home of the Chigems.'

Cathy looked at the trees. Even from their distance, the trees were tall and thin. Some looked so tall that the clouds whipped past the treetops high in the air.

They stretched far off into the distance and Cathy struggled to see beyond where Sky was pointing.

'How are we going to help them?'

'We aren't.' Sky sighed. 'You will remain with Flash and his most trusted crew. I will lead the others to free the Chigems and get you back to the safety of Painted Point.'

'I want to help.'

'Cathy, please.' Sky released a deep sigh. 'The journey inland to the far side of Spine Forest will be two more days. From there it will be a half day's journey on foot to the mines.'

'I can learn in two days.'

'If only it were that simple.' Sky placed a hand on her shoulders and turned Cathy to face him. 'We will continue your training while we journey along Rainbow River, but please agree to remain with Flash when we travel inland.'

'Why won't you let me go?'

'The Dark Queen still searches for you. Bringing you to the mines would be a temptation to her.'

'Why does she want me?'

Sky was once again uncomfortable, and it was Cathy's turn to press. Knowing that Sky's anger was still close to the surface, she proceeded with caution as she replaced the Aralcym back on her belt. Not wanting to push, she took another moment to admire the magical view of Mielikuvitus.

'I fear the Dark Queen is seeking a way to activate the Gonks-Venit.'

'What's that got to do with me?'

'I'm not sure.' Sky confessed as she twirled the tendrils of his beard with his fingers. 'I have never studied the stones. I was always of the hope that they were nothing more than a myth.'

'Is there anyone who can tell us more about them?' Cathy pressed with caution.

'Captain?' Sky suddenly boomed.

'Yes?'

'Can you send a messenger bird to Conn-Uri? I would seek an audience with Nasser.'

'Nasser?' Cathy felt a pang of excitement. 'He's still alive?'

'Very much alive, my dear Cathy. The old unicorn stills wears the scars of our war with the Dark Entity, but now lives a life of peace and solitude.'

'I shall send one immediately.' Flash sang, and Cathy heard his footsteps as he left the top deck.

'Promise me you'll listen to me, Cathy.' Sky's serious tone had returned. 'I fear evil intentions from the Dark Queen and would see you safely away from her until you are ready and prepared to face her.'

'I want to help.'

'You are helping.' Sky once again dropped to his knees in front of her. 'You being here has seen Bubus amass an armada of ships at a moment's notice. You are a beacon of hope in our world. The fact there have been whispers of the Dark Queen and now she rises from the Forgottenlands we are already stronger in facing her.'

'I don't feel like a beacon, I feel like an enormous disappointment.'

'You are nothing of the sort and should banish that doubt from your mind.' Sky moved the hair from her face and tucked it behind her ear. 'I will continue your training while we journey inland and I will show that the fire burns inside you.'

Cathy felt unconvinced. Despite knowing Sky believed in her, she could not shake the feeling she was not as good as her family, that somehow she was so far behind them that no amount of training would see her be able to do what they could. Although she had argued her point, she suddenly regretted having pressed Sky, as his expectations of her seemed even higher now.

'Can I have a minute to sort myself out?'

'What?' Sky chuckled as he rose to his feet. 'I thought you wanted to train right away.'

'Well.' A sudden outburst of laughter from Sky silenced her protest.

'Of course, get yourself ready and then join me.'

'Where?' Sky gave no answer. Instead, he simply raised his gaze to the mainmast of the ship. 'Oh, great.'

Cathy excused herself and made her way back to the hold. Grateful for Evie staying by her side, she descended the stairs and paused to speak with her.

'You were lucky.' Evie began as she jumped from midway down the staircase. 'I've seen Sky react far worse than that for lesser things. He clearly sees a lot of promise in you, even if you don't.'

'I didn't mean to upset him. I just don't want to feel so useless.'

'You're not useless and I wish you'd stop thinking it.' Evie sat at Cathy's feet and looked up at her. 'I know you expect a lot of yourself but if you're always living in someone else's shadow, you'll never be as strong as you could be.'

'But Tim could do all this easier than me. I saw what he could do when he was only just a bit older than I am now.'

'You're not Tim.' Evie interrupted. 'You're not Aiden, your dad or your mum. You're you, my Cathy, my best friend and my hero.'

'I don't feel like a hero.'

'You will, when the time is right. I can see it in your heart.'

Such a simple gesture caught Cathy by surprise as Evie rested her oversized paw above Cathy's heart. In such a tender moment, Sky watched from the top of the steps and disappeared out of sight, leaving the two friends alone.

Chapter Fifteen

Days On The Water

Cathy dripped with sweat as she climbed down the rope ladder after the second day of training. Her heart pounded, and she had long ago lost her control of the frustration rising inside her. Less than an hour ago she had been perched atop the narrow beam above the crow's nest with the Aralcym in her hand.

Balancing precariously on the smooth wooden beam, Cathy had stared at the carved dragon's head as it glinted in the sunlight. Standing in the crow's nest below, Sky had whispered to her, his voice barely rising over the sound of the whipping wind.

'Feel the warmth growing in your hand.' He had soothed, his voice seeking to guide her on a path she could not see. 'Your heart burns with the same fire as your brothers, as your parents. It is in there.'

For the first time, Cathy had felt something as Sky had spoken. The leather-bound handle in her hand was indeed warmer to the touch than she had noticed before. Clamping her eyes shut, she concentrated on the feeling and willed it to grow.

Much to her annoyance, the feeling faded and was replaced by the chill of the air that whipped across her palm as she balanced on the beam.

'I felt something.' Cathy sighed as she moved to grab the mainmast. 'But it's gone again, I can't feel it anymore.'

'Excellent!' Sky beamed, his grin burning through the salt and pepper beard. 'Try again, I know we're close.'

Cathy wanted to feel the same swell of excitement as Sky, but she didn't. Knowing Sky would not let up, she settled herself on the beam and shuffled away from the mast. Finding her balance, she once again positioned herself with the Aralcym in front of her and concentrated on the details of the dragon's head.

It was a beautiful piece of artwork. Whoever had carved the stone had done so with painstaking detail. Each scale of the dragon caught the sun and the hollow eyes seemed to bore into Cathy's soul as she looked into them. Settling her breath, she allowed her gaze to wander to the shores passing by the magnificent ship.

A movement by the banks caught her attention as a family of golden-mane unicorns trotted alongside the Lady Chance. Hoping to see Nasser, she was disappointed, but smiled at the fact she had once again been able to see the regal creatures roaming freely.

'Bring your attention back to the Aralcym.' Sky guided, his words delivered with enough sternness to remind Cathy what she was supposed to be doing.

'Sorry.'

'No need to apologise, they are beautiful creatures and seeing them lifts my spirits too.'

'Does that mean Nasser's here?' Cathy recalled the battered unicorn when she had visited Poc.

'I'd like to hope they are his entourage, yes.'

'Can we-'

'When you're done.' Sky was firm with his words, and Cathy knew what she had to do.

Looking back to the dragon's head, she turned the Aralcym around. Bringing the Jaguar's head into her line of sight, she focussed on its face before closing her eyes. Picturing the carved jaguar in her mind, she allowed the sound of the whipping wind to fade away.

Once again, after what felt like an age, the warmth returned to her hand. Not wanting to break whatever connection she had found, Cathy kept her eyes closed and focussed on the warmth. It was a strange sensation. Somehow the skin on her hand tingled as the subtle heat spread across her hand, down her fingers, and followed her veins up her forearm.

'You can feel it.' Sky announced, the excitement clear in his voice.

'How do you know?'

'I can see it in your face. Hold on to it, feed it.'

Cathy wasn't sure what "feeding it" meant, but she was determined to hold on to the sensation in her hand. Gripping the handle tighter, she dared to open her eyes and felt her mouth drop at what she saw.

The world around her seemed to move in slow-motion. The lapping water of Rainbow River slowed, and the flapping sails appeared almost still, although she knew they were moving. All that aside, it was the open mouth of the jaguar that stole all her attention as a single flame appeared like a serpent's tongue between its teeth.

'I'm doing it!'

The flame was no wider than a strand of hair, but there was no denying it was there. Staring at the flickering flame, she watched the embers fly off in the now unfelt wind that moved around her.

'Control it, make it grow into something bigger than it is. Use your will to control it.'

Staring at the flame, Cathy used every ounce of her concentration to force the fire to do something. Although she had called it from the open mouth of the jaguar, it would not listen to her silent commands. Instead, it simply remained wrapped around the sharp canine and stayed as it was.

'I can't.'

'You can.'

Feeling the sweat form on her brow, Cathy concentrated with all her efforts to force the flame to move. Despite everything, the thin fire would not listen to her commands.

'Move!' She screamed in anger, her voice carrying in the wind.

Just before the flame retracted back into the mouth, in response to her sudden scream, the flame turned its end towards her. For a split second, before it disappeared from view, the flame had listened to her. Seeing it disappear back into the depths of the open mouth, it did not fill Cathy with disappointment, but a sense of hope that she had some sort of connection to the magic held inside the Aralcym.

'That's enough.'

'I can try again.' Cathy argued and thrust the Aralcym into her eye line again.

'Don't force it, your connection is delicate.'

'I can do it.'

Cathy was about to close her eyes again when she felt Sky's hand on her foot. Looking down, she saw the soft look on Sky's face and lowered the Aralcym to her side.

'Celebrate what you've achieved today and show me you are a better student than Timothy was.'

'What do you mean by that?'

'When he was learning as you are now, I allowed him to push himself before he was ready.' Sky's face was painted with concern. 'It was a mistake that drew the Dark Entity to him sooner than I would have liked.'

'I can do it though, I know I can.'

'It's not a mistake I want to make again, Cathy.' Sky looked down at the deck below. 'We will push when it is right and not a moment before. If Sucatraps taught me anything, it's knowing when and how far to push my students.'

Knowing she could not argue, Cathy offered a nod and hooked the weapon back onto her belt. Taking hold of the mainmast, Cathy looked around and realised the Lady Chance was now steering towards the shores of Rainbow River and what appeared to be a gathering of unicorns a little way ahead of them.

Looking at the trees, Cathy realised the ship was bathed in shadow from the impossibly high canopy of Spine Forest. Craning her neck, Cathy could see the lower branches, but most of the oversized trees touched the clouds high above. Never in her life had Cathy seen a tree so enormous as the ones that now surrounded the ship.

'Is this our last stop before the mines?' Cathy quizzed as she descended the rope ladders back down to the deck.

The Lady Chance was anchored by the riverbanks as the sun disappeared behind the trees. Although the sky was still bright, the river itself was dark as if it were night, as the giant trees obscured the sun completely. Feeling a fresh chill in the air, Cathy waited as they lowered a gangplank into position, allowing her access to the comfort of land.

Eager to no longer feel the sway of the ship, Cathy was first to hoist herself onto the narrow wooden plank and jog down to solid ground. Hot on her heels, Evie followed, as ever, by her side as a companion and protector.

'It cannot be!' A familiar voice exclaimed from behind a crescent of golden-mane unicorns.

As the unicorns parted, a sight she had never expected to see greeted Cathy. Although Nasser could take the form of a unicorn, he had long since abandoned transformation back into his equestrian form. He was a lot older than Cathy remembered, his hair now pale white and he sported a curious attempt at a beard, well more sideburns that hung down past his shoulders.

'Nasser.' Cathy beamed and stood proudly by Evie's side.

'You cannot be the young girl I remember, surely not.'

Nasser walked with a cane and Cathy struggled not to look to the crooked stump where his impressive horn had once stood. She recalled the first time she had seen the regal leader of the unicorns touching death, having been attacked by the Croinsop. He had fought alongside her family in the great battle against the Dark Entity and had always appeared kind to Cathy.

'It's been so long.'

Cathy hesitated, wanting to hug him, but wasn't sure of traditions and expectations. As Nasser limped over to her, he was quick to allay her fears as he wrapped his free arm around her and held her in a warm hug.

'I'm both saddened and happy you're here, my sweet Cathy Scott.'

'Why are you sad?'

'Because, my dear, Sky has told me how you came to be here and speaks of the Dark Queen's search for the Gonks-Venit.'

'Is it really that bad?'

Nasser paused before answering as he looked up to see Sky descending the gangplank towards them. His mood changed in an instant as he released Cathy and took a step back to lean on his walking stick.

'It's worse than bad, Cathy.' Nasser hushed as Sky joined them. 'My dear Sky, why is it that every time the darkness appears, you need my help.'

'Because, old friend, we are always the first line of defence in protecting the peace and tranquillity of Mielikuvitus. Even if you are almost too old to be of use.'

Both men laughed and shared an embrace. Taking the time to look around, Cathy saw Captain Flash watching from the top deck as the remaining ships of the vast armada dropped anchor behind the Lady Chance.

Despite being unable to go to the mines, Cathy knew Sky and Bubus had amassed a sizeable army to fight back the Dark Queen's soldiers. For the first time since sneaking aboard the Lady Chance, Cathy saw the eight Chigems marching down the gangplank, their footfalls once again in unison.

Once again she fought to suppress the laughter that bubbled inside at the comical movement of the

Chigem's oversized arms as they marched down towards her.

'We feast and draw plans.' Flash announced from the ship. 'My crew will serve a feast of battle, as is our tradition.'

Cathy watched as the crew of the Lady Chance erupted into action. Joined by the Chigems, Cathy felt somewhat ousted by the conversations and planning that filled the early parts of the evening. Taking time to find a place of isolation with Evie, the two of them stared at the shimmering surface of Rainbow River and enjoyed some time alone together.

CHAPTER SIXTEEN

MATTERS WORSE

'Cathy, come quick.'

The voice quickly broke through the dream she had been having, and Cathy sat bolt upright. After their time alone, Cathy had returned to the Lady Chance and found comfort in a hammock suspended beneath the bowsprit. Searching out the source of the voice, Cathy struggled for a moment before she found on the Chigems perched on the railing above her.

Wiping the sleep from her eyes, Cathy fought the urge to laugh at the comical arms protruding from the feathered chicken's chest. Composing herself, Cathy hoisted herself onto the bowsprit and moved back onto the deck.

'What's happening?'

'Master Sky needs you, something's happened at the mines.'

Clarice's voice was shrill with fear and as Cathy looked beyond the ship and saw an enormous plume of thick black smoke rising into the air. With no chance to ask questions, Clarice ran off across the deck and down the gangplank.

Taking the Chigem's lead, Cathy followed behind and was glad to see Evie already with Sky and the gathering of captains from the anchored ships.

'Ah, Cathy.' Sky waved to her as she balanced down the plank. 'We've had news from the mines. We must move at once.'

'Am I going with you?' It was hard for Cathy to hide her excitement at the prospect, but Sky's stern glare quickly quashed that.

'Nothing has changed about you being here.' Sky warned. 'You're going to stay right here on the Lady Chance with Captain Flash and a handful of his crew.'

'But-'

'Without argument.' Sky interrupted.

'When we saw the smoke, I sent three of our sisters to see what has happened.' Clarice added, breaking the tension between Cathy and Sky.

'And what have they found out?' Cathy pressed.

'The mines are burning, the Dark Queen's trolls have started marching out.' Rex was breathless as she trotted from the treeline flanked by Ethal and Jade.

'Any sign of the Dark Queen?' Sky asked as he moved aside, allowing the returning Chigems past.

'Nothing.' Jade used her oversized hand to flatten the feathers atop her head. 'But we didn't stay long enough to look too much.'

'And the Gonks-Venit?' It was Nasser who spoke as he stood on the deck of the Lady Chance looking down at the gathering. 'Did you see anything that would say she has found them in the mines?'

'We didn't see anything.'

Sky stormed past Cathy and stalked back up the gangplank to speak with Nasser. The two of them were animated in their conversation, but kept it quiet enough that Cathy and the others could not hear what was being said.

'What's got them so upset?' Cathy hushed at Evie as she moved to sit by her side.

'I suspect it is the worry if the gems have been found.' Clarice answered as she hopped to stand on a tree stump in front of Cathy.

'Do you think she did, find them I mean?'

'I hope not.'

'Are they really that dangerous? Do you think she could do what Sky was talking about, bringing the worlds together?'

'The Gonks-Venit are one piece of the puzzle.' Nasser interrupted as he hobbled down the gangplank. 'The thing that concerns me the most is that we know nothing about the other pieces. If the Dark Queen has gained them, I fear we will chase her down a path with no knowledge of where it leads.'

'We march at once.' Sky declared. 'The longer we wait, the more Chigems may fall to the trolls.'

Cathy could only watch as Sky gathered the crew of the accompanying ships and prepared to march for the Chigem mines. Feeling somewhat of a spare part, Cathy returned to the Lady Chance and sat herself on the steps leading to the top deck.

After what felt like an age, Sky announced his presence with a subtle cough and waited for Cathy to look up at him.

'You are best here with Flash.' Sky began as he took a seat beside her on the steps. 'I know you want to help, but without knowing what the Dark Queen plans, I won't let you risk being taken by her.'

'I know you're right, but it doesn't mean I have to like it.'

'I'd be disappointed if you just sat there and accepted it, Cathy.' Sky chuckled. 'Your spirit is what makes you strong, your willingness to press ahead despite everything.'

'Then let me go?' She offered a coy smile as she spoke. 'I had to at least try.'

'That you did, my dear.' Sky ruffled her hair as he stood. 'Keep practising while I'm gone and when I'm back, we will conjure more than just a tendril, I promise you.'

'How long do you think you'll be gone?'

'Three days, maybe four and we should be back.' There was a slight hesitation in Sky's answer, but Cathy chose not to press.

'I'll be waiting.'

It was enough of a promise to satisfy Sky, as he offered a simple nod and left Cathy once again alone on the deck. Peeking through the railings, Cathy watched as Sky gathered the cohorts of soldiers and sailors and disappeared into Spine Forest. Seeing the last of the array of creatures disappear amongst the thick trunks of the giant trees.

Cathy remained sat on the steps for the rest of the afternoon. Evie watched from across the deck, feigning sleep but keep her eyes on Cathy all the while. Once the sun had dipped behind the horizon and the ship was bathed in the red glow of the dying sun, the crew became visible again.

'Mind if I join you?' Flash's voice caught Cathy by surprise as she had started to doze with her head resting against the step.

'Sure.' Her answer was noncommittal and Flash eyed her for a moment.

'What worries you Cathy Scott?' Flash asked as he licked the back of his paw and flattened his ear down. 'I see your face filled with frustration.'

'I feel useless.' Cathy groaned, not in the mood to talk but knowing Flash was looking out for her, she felt it was only right to answer.

'You are far from useless Cathy Scott.' Flash corrected as he cleaned himself. 'Simply being aboard the Lady Chance has given hope to my crew. The whisper of your name was enough to bring the Chigems calling for help.'

'More like they thought my brother was here, not me.' Cathy stood and walked to the back of the glorious ship. 'Imagine how disappointed they would have been when they saw little old me instead.'

Cathy toyed with the ship's wheel as Flash watched from the top of the staircase. Despite his human appearance, Flash was still very much a cat as he rested a leg against the railing and licked the length of his furry leg.

'You are far too hard on yourself.' Flash explained between lengthy licks of his leg. 'You should remember who you are and stop comparing yourself to your family.'

'Easy for you to say.'

Cathy looked beyond Flash and admired the crew as they worked at securing the enormous sails and fixing the rigging ropes that hung from the various masts. Seeing the feline crew bouncing and swinging between the sails was a sight to behold and yet Cathy still felt distracted at the thought of Sky marching to the mines without her.

Having resigned herself to remaining on the Lady Chance, Cathy was about to speak when a sudden movement above the ship caught her eye. Resting against the ship's wheel, Cathy covered her eyes and scanned beyond the mainmast.

'What's that?'

Pointing skyward, Flash moved to her side and looked up towards the sky.

'What is it?'

'Something was flying above the ship, it looked like a big bird.'

'There shouldn't be anything out here, the Spine Forest is too tall for anything to grow, and besides-' Flash stopped mid-sentence as he too caught sight of movement.

Craning his neck, Flash covered his eyes to see what he was looking at but it was Evie who knew something was amiss. Releasing a piercing howl, she launched herself onto all fours and sniffed the air.

The whole crew fell silent and looked at Evie. Her nose pointing towards the star-filled sky and canopy of trees, she took a long inhale and Cathy watched her fur bristle.

'Below deck,' Evie snarled, her top lip lifting to show her canines. 'Get below deck Cathy.'

'What's going on?'

'Now!' Evie barked.

Before Cathy could take a step, the flying creature dropped from above and somersaulted in the air to land with a thump on the deck between Cathy and Evie. Shocked by the sudden arrival, Cathy was about to speak when one by one a dozen more of the strange creatures landed on the deck of the Lady Chance.

Cathy stared at the nearest of the creatures and took in its appearance. The flying creature was some sort of gargoyle, its skin looking like stone with bulbous features and awkward angles. Turning to face her, Cathy caught sight the devilish eyes that glared at her from the chiselled stone face.

'The girl, there she is.'

Pointing its stone finger at Cathy, she felt a shudder down her spine as another of the gargoyles crashed onto the deck behind her. Reacting just in time she dodged the creature's attempt to grab her and sprinted across the deck.

In a heartbeat, Flash withdrew a pair of his swords and took his place between Cathy and the gargoyle.

'Get to Evie, get below deck. We will keep you safe.'

Flash attacked before giving Cathy a chance to respond and suddenly the deck of the Lady Chance was a flurry of battling as the crew dropped from the masts and set about giving Cathy the chance to make her escape.

Ducking and dodging, Cathy launched herself from the top deck and felt her fall broken by Evie's soft coat. Bouncing to the deck, she snatched the Aralcym from her side and willed something to happen. Glaring at the stone figure in her hand, Cathy snatched a discarded sword from the deck as another of the gargoyles launched at her.

Thrusting the sword up, the blade sparked as it scraped across the rough surface of the gargoyle's arm and it yelped in shock at the sudden defence. Taking advantage of the distraction, Cathy rolled herself away and sprinted to the doorway to the ship's hold.

Evie was close by her side as the air was filled with a feeling of electricity as an enormous crash of thunder rocked every plank and screw on the ship. Stopping in her tracks, Cathy turned to find the source of the storm as a bolt of lightning crashed down from the clouds and collided with the main deck.

Wood and metal exploded from the deck forcing Cathy to shield her face. Once the debris had finished crashing, she uncovered her face and gasped as the Dark Queen stood tall and regal where the lightning bolt had struck. Splintered wood smouldered at her feet as she stood tall, staring at Cathy, her blue hair crackling with sparks of electricity.

'Nobody needs to get hurt.' Her words were thunderous and laced with sinister warning. 'Give yourself to me and I will spare your friends.'

Clapping her hands, the gargoyles took advantage of the distraction and in a matter of seconds almost the entire crew were locked in the stone arms of the gargoyles. With no idea what to do, Cathy looked around in desperation as Evie launched through the air and placed herself between the Dark Queen and Cathy.

'She's going nowhere with you.' Evie growled and sank her claws into the wood.

'Stand aside.' The Dark Queen warned as she raised her hand in front of her face.

'No.'

Without warning, with no threat or words, the Dark Queen launched a bolt of lightning that stretched the length of her arm and exploded through the air towards Evie. Before Cathy could even speak a word, she felt herself launched through the air as the bolt of electricity collided with Evie.

As both Cathy and Evie were thrown through the air, Cathy felt herself crash into the ship's wheel that snapped in half with her weight. Dropping to the deck her body screamed with pain but she had something else to worry about. Dragging herself to the edge, she peered between the railings and saw Evie lying on her side, eyes open and chest no longer moving.

As the pain shut down Cathy's sense, the last thing she remembered were the spark of electricity that danced across Evie's lifeless body on the deck below. As unconsciousness swallowed her, Cathy felt her heart break in her chest and, for the first time in as long as she could remember, she felt utterly lost and without anyone to help her. She was broken.

CHAPTER SEVENTEEN

PRISONER AGAIN

Cathy awoke with a start as a loud bang echoed along the hallway outside the cell door. Eyes wide she scanned around the room and felt dismay to see someone had shackled her ankles.

'I hate this place,' she groaned as her hands tugged at the rusted metal.

Feeling the rough metal digging into her hands, Cathy released the shackles and pressed her head against the cold stone wall. The sudden realisation of what had happened to Evie hit her like a shock-wave. From nowhere her eyes filled with tears and she wept at the memory of her friend lying on the deck of the Lady Chance, eyes open and lifeless.

In the dimly lit cell, the only light coming in through a narrow window near the ceiling, Cathy was left alone as she wallowed in the memory of Evie. This wasn't her first loss in Mielikuvitus, the only two times she had crossed through the mirror she had suffered pain and loss. It was not lost on her that although she had longed to return, this place only brought sadness and grief with each visit.

'I want to go home.' Was also she could mutter between sharp intakes of breath as she fought back against the flowing tears.

'Maybe I can help you with that.' The Dark Queen's voice surprised her and Cathy scanned the small cell in search of the voice's source.

Seeing she was still alone, Cathy rose to her feet and shuffled towards the large door blocking her path into the hallway beyond. Her only view of the hallway came from a narrow opening that she pressed her face towards to see out of the door.

As soon as her eyes adjusted to the light behind the door, she saw the Dark Queen standing in front of her.

'You slept for longer than I would have expected.' The Dark Queen mocked as she stood like a statue on the far side of the hallway. 'That's to be expected from such a young and uninitiated little girl.'

Cathy took a moment to compose herself. As much as it pained her, she pushed aside the memories of Evie and Minnie and glared through the narrow gap at the regal Queen. Standing tall there was no denying she carried herself with an air of grace and prowess.

Before speaking, Cathy took in the full glory of the armoured dress the Dark Queen wore. The chest plate was adorned with a winding snake that stretched around her torso and ended with a snake's mouth in mid attack near her shoulder. A high ruffled collar framed around her slender neck and the shocking head of electric blue hair drew Cathy's attention to her face.

There was something cold about her sinister eyes that stared at her across the hall. Breaking her gaze, Cathy admired the flowing skirt but felt no doubt the Queen's clothes while regal in appearance had been designed for battle. The shimmering chest plate all but confirmed her suspicions on its own.

'Nothing to say young Cathy Scott?'

'Not to you.' Cathy bit back, her anger and hatred seeping through in her retort.

'Disappointing.' As she spoke, the Dark Queen sounded like a disappointed teacher chastising a student. 'I had hoped to offer you a way home without any more suffering.'

Despite herself, Cathy knew her reaction gave away the steely resolve she was trying to portray. More than anything she wanted to hug her mother and rest her head in her lap. Whenever things turned dark it was always her mum who she felt safest going to. Her dad, of course, had his merits but he was a lot like Timothy and unable to express his emotions. Her dad was always someone she would turn to when she needed a smile, always playful and joking but right now she needed her mum.

'My offer intrigues you?' The Dark Queen pressed delicately, careful not to push Cathy too much.

Stepping away from the door, Cathy turned her back on the door but felt the Dark Queens gaze all the same. Looking up to the narrow window just beneath the cell's ceiling she looked to the blue sky and clouds.

Composing herself, Cathy kept her back to the door and tried to come up with the best answer. Before she could speak, the door behind her rattled and she turned to see one of the bulbous trolls push the door open.

'Come with me.' The troll droned as it pointed its finger to the floor in front of him.

Reluctant at first, Cathy watched as the Dark Queen turned away from the cell and stalked away, the sound of her footfalls fading away into the distance. Remaining defiant, fighting back the floods of tears that welled in her eyes, Cathy shoved her hands into the pockets of her now dirt-stained dress and recoiled a little as she felt a clump of Evie's fur in the depths of the pocket.

'What happened to my friends?'

'The pitiful cats on the ship?' The troll snapped as it shuffled into the cell. 'Her highness saw fit to leave them be once she reclaimed you.'

'Good.' Cathy sighed as the troll set about releasing the shackles around her ankles and quickly bound her hands in front of her.

'Of course, they won't be returning to that pitiful place they call home anytime soon.'

'What do you mean?'

'Her highness sank the ships and left a squadron of her finest soldiers to greet the dirty Elder Sky upon his return from the mines.'

A fresh wave of anger welled inside Cathy as she fought to rip her cuffed hands free from the troll's grasp. Outmatched against the bulbous troll's strength it was a pointless venture as the large creature simply lifted Cathy into the air and hoisted her over his armoured shoulder.

'Let's not make this any harder than it needs to be young one.'

With no choice but to allow herself to be carried from the cell, Cathy went limp and hung over the trolls shoulder as he carried her through the labyrinth of the Dark Queen's Palace. It was not long before Cathy found herself emerging onto a tremendous balcony that overlooked the barren landscape of the Forgottenlands.

'Leave us.' The Dark Queen announced as the troll lowered Cathy to the ground.

With her hands bound by the metal chains around her wrists, Cathy moved to the edge of the balcony and felt her stomach turn as she realised how high above the ground she was. Looking down, the rows of marching trolls looked like nothing more than ants on a play mat. Stepping away from the edge, Cathy lifted her gaze to the distant horizon and realised how busy the Dark Queen had been in her exile in the Forgottenlands.

All Cathy had ever heard about the Forgottenlands had led her to believe it was a lifeless and empty place. Looking out from the Palace, it was far from a lifeless barren landscape that stretched out in front of her. The Dark Queen had constructed a city to rival Partum in its size and expanse and where the Table of Haras dominated Partum's centre, the focal point of this place was something very different.

'My arena.' The Dark Queen announced as she moved to stand by Cathy's side.

'What do you want from me?' Cathy asked as the Queen rested her hands on the balcony's edge and admired her creation.

'Only the same as what you long for.' The Dark Queen's riddled answer made no sense. 'You seek a way home and I offer it to you.'

'Really?' Cathy's words were laced with disbelief. 'You'd just send me home and that would be the end of it?'

'I never said that.' The Queen chuckled. 'You will open the ancient portals and our world will once again be united as they were at the time of creation.'

'I won't do it.' Cathy declared in defiance.

'You would live the rest of your meaningless life as my prisoner, never to be held close by your mother?'

The mention of Cathy's family had the desired effect and while the Dark Queen knew the look on Cathy's face, she kept her attention on the sprawling city. As Cathy fought to find an answer that would at least sound truthful, she fought to look beyond the Dark Queen and drag her struggling brain off the track of fear the Queen was setting her on.

'Where are the Croinsop?'

'Those vile creatures?' The Dark Queen spat her reply as she turned on the spot and glared at Cathy. 'They served their purpose for the Dark Entity in the past, but when true power offered them a hand they turned through fear.'

'You think you are true power?' Cathy stifled her smirk and saw the Dark Queen's face twitch with frustration.

'The trolls answered my call, as did a handful of the vile Croinsop and other creatures of the Forgottenlands who realised the truth.'

'What truth would that be then?'

'The truth that I will be powerful enough to unite our worlds and rid it of weakness.'

Realising the tables had turned, Cathy feigned amusement and felt pleasure as the Dark Queen fought to quell her own frustration. Although Cathy's fears and loss still swam dangerously close to the surface, seeing the Queen on the defence gave her a glimmer of satisfaction as she pressed further.

'For all those that joined you, doesn't it tell you something if even more turned away from you? I mean, the Croinsop were fearsome warriors when they fought alongside the Dark Entity and yet they turned away from you.'

Cathy had always been like this with her brothers. Despite Timothy and Aiden being older than her, she had always had a way of winning arguments with them by sowing seeds of doubt in themselves and their arguments. Well-versed and skilled, even at eleven, Cathy knew she had caught the Dark Queen by surprise.

'You know nothing.' The Dark Queen snarled as she ripped Cathy's Aralcym from a small table by her side. 'You are a pathetic little girl who desperately longs to see her mummy and daddy because everything she knows is dead.'

Once again the realisation hit Cathy like a wall and she felt the air ripped from her lungs. Having turned the tables, the Dark Queen was not quick to ease her onslaught and took the handful of steps to stand towering over Cathy.

'Shut up.'

'Funny.' The Dark Queen sniggered. 'Having your own weaknesses highlighted leaves you a cowering mess, not worthy of a presence before the mighty Dark Queen.'

'I won't help you.' Cathy stammered as she wiped the tears from her face. 'You can do what you want to me, I'm not going to give in to you.'

Dropping to her knees, the Dark Queen held her face close to Cathy's Reaching out her slender hand she stole a tear from Cathy's cheek and admired it in the bright sunlight. As the teardrop threatened to tumble to the ground, the Dark Queen moved her hand to keep the single droplet of water rolling around her hand until it finished in her palm.

'I actually believe you.' She murmured as she squashed the tear in her clenched fist. 'Perhaps appealing to your pain and loss is not the right way to go about it.'

'What are you going to do?'

'Guards!' The Queen disregarded Cathy as she turned and stalked towards the open archway leading back into the Palace.

'Your Highness?' A gargoyle questioned as it dropped onto the balcony.

'Take her to the arena.' The Dark Queen offered Cathy a menacing smile. 'If the loss of her friends and family don't convince her to help me, maybe the risk of her own life being stolen will be enough.'

Before she could say a word, Cathy was hoisted into the air as the gargoyle creature launched over the edge of the balcony and flew her above the city towards the impressive arena. Fighting not to scream, Cathy dug her fingers into the stony hands that held her in place as the ground whipped by below them.

Chapter Eighteen

The Dark Queen's Offer

The gargoyle dropped Cathy in the centre of the immense arena. It was like nothing she had seen before and yet, somehow, it felt familiar. Cathy had seen something similar in her history books at school about the Romans and Greeks but they were simple buildings, nothing like the ornate building she found herself in the centre of now.

A series of jagged spires protruded from the ground almost looking like an upturned spider. Between the legs sat rows of seats that looked like hammocks suspended between thin struts. In a way the entire building looked like cobwebs and spider's legs and it sent a coarse chill down Cathy's spine.

For the longest time she was alone in the centre of the arena. The wind swept through the rows of suspended hammocks and set them swaying but aside from the whistle of the wind, nothing stirred.

'Hello?' Cathy asked, her voice echoing around the vast arena.

When she found herself unanswered, Cathy dared to move around the dusty arena floor and moved towards a trio of tall columns of stone that protruded from the floor. Moving closer, Cathy realised the nearest of two of the stone were etched with lines, one completely filled on all sides top to bottom. The second, however was only half filled with the notches of battle.

Moving to stand in front of the central column, Cathy pressed her hands against the rough surface and jumped as a voice interrupted her thoughts.

'The latest offering from the Queen?'

The voice was haggard, old and gruff. Turning around, Cathy gasped as she found herself still alone in the centre of the arena, no sign of the person that had spoken to her.

'Another one that'll last a few minutes.' The voice teased. 'Can't even see what's right in front of it.'

Spinning around Cathy looked every which way for the source of the voice but still saw nothing. Awash with frustration, Cathy was about to speak again when a handful of coarse sand was thrown into her face.

Recoiling from the sudden attack, Cathy felt the grains of sand in her mouth and spat out a mix of spit and ground as she wiped the dirt from her eyes.

'Hey, stop that.'

'Why, you're the one who can't see what's right in front of her.'

A second handful of sand splashed into her face, sending her stumbling backwards to crash to the floor. Frustrated and spitting out another mouthful of dirt and sand, she scooped up a handful herself and threw it out in front of her. Hitting nothing, the handful of sand splashed onto the surface of the nearest column.

'Where are you?' Cathy yelled in frustration as she scooped up another handful of dirt.

'Open your eyes and look-'

The goading was cut short as Cathy tossed the handful of sand in the direction of the voice. Colliding with something, the small creature that hovered in front of her suddenly crashed to the floor. As the creature slammed into the floor, Cathy was on it in an instant and grabbed it around whatever body part she could feel.

'Let me go.' The voice shrieked but Cathy held it tight in her hands.

'Who are you?'

'Let me go.'

'Tell me who you are.'

Cathy could feel beating wings on the back of her hands but refused to let go. Fighting against the surprising strength, Cathy pulled the invisible creature closer to her and at least it revealed itself to her.

As soon as she saw the familiar pastel-coloured skin and hair she let go of her grip on the Ecilop and allowed it to fly away from her. Looking strikingly familiar to Tim's Ecilop, Aleobe, Cathy could not believe one of their kind would be here and apparently in service to the Dark Queen.

'Feel better now?' The Ecilop spat as it flew to the top of the central column to sit on the crumbling edge.

'What is an Ecilop doing here? I mean, well, why? I thought you were on our side.'

'Our side?'

'We're setting off on the wrong foot, sorry, my name is Cathy Scott and you are?'

For a moment the Ecilop sat perched on the ledge, its head buried in its little hands. After what felt like a lifetime, the Ecilop looked down at Cathy and dropped down to fly in front of her.

'My name is Dux and I know who you are, Cathy Scott.'

'How do you know me?'

'Because my older brother is Aleobe, your brother's friend.'

Cathy was flabbergasted at the revelation as a thousand questions raced through her head.

'But why are you here?'

'Not all of us are lucky enough to find ourselves living by the side of a Partum Spiritus and Aleobe, he was always the favourite.' There was a sadness on Dux' face as he hovered in front of Cathy. 'I left home in search of a friend and found Laddie, long after he became home of the Dark Entity.'

'You shouldn't be here, this isn't a place for you.'

'Isn't it?' Dux' expression changed as he dusted off the sand from his shoulders and launched up into the air. 'This is the only place in the whole of my world where I can be something.'

'What is this place to you?'

'This is the Dark Queen's arena and I am the Master of Ceremonies.' There was a glee and pride in his voice now and he flew around the entire arena floor leaving a cloud of dust behind him. 'It is my voice that stirs the crowds, my words that launch the games and bring everyone together under my roof.'

'What would your brother say to that?'

'My brother doesn't care.' Dux bellowed as he took his position above the central column. 'If he had cared, he would have come for me when I first left Poc. Nobody cared, they left me be and just like Laddie I found my new home.'

Tapping his foot on the column, Cathy gasped as all three stone structures slowly descended into the floor.

As it did, the arena was filled with the sound of voices and chanting. Turning around, Cathy gasped as the mass of hanging hammock seats slowly filled with creatures of every shape and size ranging from trolls, gargoyles and Croinsop to many she did not recognise.

'My servants.' The Dark Queen's voice echoed in the air as she appeared on the sinking stone column beside Dux. 'Welcome to the Grand Arena.'

A sea of applause filled the air as the Dark Queen came to rest in front of Cathy. Raising her hands to the air, she drank in the applause and allowed it to consume her for a moment before she urged her servants to fall silent.

'All Hail the Queen of the Forgottenlands.' Dux announced as he moved to sit on the Dark Queen's shoulder.

There was something unnerving and perverse seeing an Ecilop so close to a woman of darkness and evil. Cathy remembered the delight and joy on her brother's face with his companionship with Aleobe and yet seeing the Dark Queen with her own seemed out of place and wrong.

'As you can see Cathy, I bring together all creatures of Mielikuvitus. Unlike those in Partum who would have you believe they are all welcoming, they still choose to ignore the rights and honours of those outside of their beliefs. They are no different from the Dark Entity.'

'Neither are you!' Cathy spat with venom.

'I am entirely different than him.' The Dark Queen's voice boomed. 'The Dark Entity was a vile perversion of darkness, unable to control his own desires until all he could do was consume a creature stained only with grief.'

'And what are you, if not the same vessel as Laddie was.'

The crowd fell silent, Cathy could have heard a pin drop as the Dark Queen ambled towards her.

'Laddie was nothing more than a channel for the darkness, is it any wonder the form the Dark Entity took was destined to fail? Too weak to harness its true power.' She spoke her words with great care as she sauntered around Cathy with regal poise. 'I am no vessel for the darkness, the darkness did not call to me. I called to it.'

Making her declaration, the Dark Queen raised her hands to the sky and in response the bright sun became shrouded behind a layer of thick black cloud. Lighting crackled between the clouds at her command and Cathy watched as single bolt of lightning spat from the clouds to land in the Dark Queen's upturned hand.

'What do you mean?' Cathy's voice quivered.

'I was not born to allow the darkness to take me. The tendrils of what was left when your family banished the Entity answered my call. It was my own mother who taught me to harness it, bend it to my will rather than bend myself to its.'

The Dark Queen toyed with the ball of electricity that sparked in her hand.

'You're mad.'

'No, I am far from mad. When my father turned away from my mother, it was her who raised me in the image of true power. To fill the void left behind after the Dark Entity was too weak to fulfil its destiny. A destiny you will now help me realise.'

'No I won't.'

'I offer you the chance to return to your family.'

'You offer me a chance to die with them rather than die here, alone.' Cathy retorted, tugging at the solid shackles on her wrists. 'If I help you, then everything I know will come to an end. If I don't, then it's only my end that happens.'

'And you're willing to make that sacrifice?'

'Yes.' Despite her proclamation, Cathy wasn't entirely sure she was convincing enough.

'Then let us test that resolve, young Cathy Scott.'

'The Queen gives us games.' Dux announced as he somersaulted off her shoulder. 'Bring forward the first offerings and see if this little girl can provide you anything in the way of entertainment.'

'That's not fair!' Cathy declared as she held her bound hands out to Dux and the Queen.

'You're right.' The Dark Queen smirked. 'Release her bonds, and give her companions to fight alongside.'

As the Dark Queen sauntered towards her viewing area on the far side of the arena, Cathy felt her heart sink as a handful of the Lady Chance's grew were marched into the arena. She saw how battered and broken they were and felt a pang of guilt as Captain Flash was among them, his fur matted with blood and left arm bound in bandages.

'My lady!' Flash beamed as the escorting trolls prodded them into position.

Once the dozen or so prisoners were gathered in the centre of the arena, one of the trolls emptied a sack of blunt and battered weapons onto the ground.

'Make the best of those, before you die.' The troll goaded as it made its way back towards the open gate he had ushered the prisoners out of.

'Cathy.' The Dark Queen bellowed from her viewing platform. 'I doubt you'll need it, but perhaps you'd like this.'

Cathy watched as the Dark Queen dropped her Aralcym handle onto the arena floor. As the carved weapon touched the sand, the shackles around her wrists fell free. A terrifying roar filled the air as a series of gates were lifted open in the side walls of the arena. Not wasting a moment, Cathy launched herself from the crowd of prisoners, snatching a sword as she did, and raced towards the discarded Aralcym.

The arena was filled with cheers and excitement as the games began.

CHAPTER NINETEEN

ARENA

Cathy could see the Aralcym handle resting in the sand just within reach, when a figure stepped into her path. Overcome with terror, Cathy found herself in the shadow of a Croinsop, armed with a pair of large axes.

Not giving Cathy a chance to slow, the Croinsop attacked and swiped both the axes out towards Cathy. Dropping, she skidded across the sand and felt the blades as they crossed barely a centimetre from her face. Propelled by her momentum, Cathy rolled between the open legs of the Croinsop and crashed into some sort of forward roll to land within reach of the Aralcym.

Knowing the Croinsop would be on her, Cathy snatched up the handle and turned in time to see the scorpion-like creature growling with frustration.

It's pincers clicked above its head as it wielded the axes in two of its four arms. Launching itself into the air, the Croinsop attacked and Cathy prepared to defend herself.

'Move!'

Flash pounced with agility to Cathy's side and crashed into the Croinsop's side, sending it slamming into the arena wall. As Cathy righted herself, she watched as Flash somehow defended himself against the onslaught of the Croinsop. They were, in Cathy's eyes, matched in skill and prowess as each of them fought and parried against the other's attack.

Flash kept the Croinsop at bay with his feline agility. His lightfooted manoeuvres kept him out of the Croinsop's reach, bouncing and ducking with impossible speed to keep the enormous creature guessing.

At last, the Croinsop thwarted another of Flash's parries and slammed the handle of one axe hard into his stomach. Caught in mid-flight, the power of the attack stopped Flash in flight and threw him hard against the arena wall. Knowing Flash would be winded, Cathy tightened her grip on the sword she had taken and dived towards the Croinsop.

Screams and cries of excitement filled the air all around, but Cathy registered none of it. Nothing existed between her and the fight as she bore down on the Croinsop. Her attack was expected, the Croinsop levelled an axe in her direction while never taking its attention off Flash who was now pinned against the wall.

'Flash.' Cathy hollered as she dodged away from the outstretched axe.

Unable to keep Flash pinned while holding Cathy at bay, the Croinsop released Flash and turned its attention to Cathy. Whereas it had nonchalantly tried to hold her at bay, she had now stolen its attention enough to give Flash a chance to catch his breath.

Cathy blocked the first attack, feeling herself thrown backwards by the sheer strength of the swinging axe. Digging her heels into the sand, she stopped herself from falling back, but felt herself crash into something. Looking over her shoulder, Cathy shrieked as she found herself entangled with a second Croinsop who had been focussed on one of Flash's crew.

The Croinsop looked different from the other, this one was battle-scarred and missing both pincers from above its head. Interrupted by Cathy's collision, the Croinsop turned and released an unearthly scream.

Cathy tried to back away but only made it two steps before the Croinsop wrapped a crooked hand around her neck and lifted Cathy into the air. Dragging her close to its face, Cathy could smell the putrid smell from its tough flesh as it sniffed across her face. It was only then that Cathy realised the Croinsop was blind. Someone had gouged both eyes out from its face.

Terrified at the battle-worn creature's appearance, Cathy dropped the sword and fought against the tight grip around her neck. Hanging in the air, she kicked and thrashed, but found no purchase on the spindly fingers that continued to tighten around her throat.

'Flash, help.' Her voice was dangerously quiet and she wasn't sure it had carried over the excited chatter from the crowds.

As she tried to scream again, Cathy felt the air struggling to pass down her throat, and the world started to darken around her. Desperate and afraid she would soon be unconscious, Cathy kicked and fought, but could feel her senses fading.

Staring at the scarred scorpion face that snarled at her, she closed her eyes and tried her best concentrate. Despite the screaming of the crowds and the venomous hiss of the Croinsop's laboured breaths, she pictured herself on the Lady Chance.

It was all she could think of doing, the only thing she expected Sky would tell her to do if he were there. Fighting to drown everything out, Cathy let her right hand drop to her side and touched her fingers to the leather-bound handle of the Aralcym. It was instinct, more a hope of something than any plan, but Cathy felt comfort as she touched the handle, despite her body screaming for air.

'I can do this.' She hushed to herself as she wrapped her hand around the handle.

The leather felt cold to the touch, nothing like it had when she had called the tendril of flame from the open mouth balancing on the masts of the ship. The Aralcym once again felt like it was nothing more than an ornament, some decorative item that hung at her side for no other reason than posterity.

'Such a pity.' The Croinsop snarled, its face so close that Cathy could feel the moist breath on her face. 'I had hoped one of the Partum would have returned, not a silly little girl.'

The words rang true in Cathy's ears, but filled her with anger and frustration. Opening her eyes, she was about to scream in protest when she felt a familiar warmth against her palm. Not wanting to lose her connection with the Eternal Flame and the Aralcym, Cathy ripped it from her side and drove the Aralcym upwards.

To her surprise, the Croinsop released its grip on her throat and Cathy fell with a thud to the floor. Before her eyes, the Croinsop shuddered and Cathy was covered in a spray of thick black liquid as a serrated blade burst out of its chest.

Much to her relief, Cathy watched on as the Croinsop was cut in half and fell lifeless to the floor. Standing with a bloodstained sword in its hand was one of Flash's crew and before Cathy could offer her thanks, one of the gargoyle creatures barrelled into the crewmate, sending him spinning away from her.

Although Cathy was relieved to see the Croinsop defeated, it was not lost on her that once again, Cathy had failed to call the Eternal Flame. Catching her breath, Cathy took a second to look around and saw the sea of fighting that filled the vast arena.

Her heart sank as she saw a handful of the Lady Chance's crew dead or dying on the sand while others battled with the array of creatures sent by the Dark Queen. Cathy recognised the Croinsop and gargoyles, but there were also other creatures she did not recognise. One in particular sent an icy chill down her spine.

The creature was like nothing she had seen before, all black skin and silver spikes on something that resembled a cross between a dog and a reptile. The oily black skin shimmered in the light, while four pink eyes sat low above a wide mouth filled with razor-sharp teeth. Moving on all fours, its movements seemed almost fluid as the creature stalked around a trio of the Lady Chance's crew as they stood back-to-back with their weapons outstretched.

Cathy watched the hunting creature as it sniffed the air around the trio of crewmates. Its slender tail whipped through the air and Cathy could not help but notice the large, crooked silver spikes protruding from the end of its tail. As Cathy looked on, she realised the creature, what it was, resembled some sort of dinosaur but had no time to further think as it attacked.

With impossible speed, the creature swiped its tail through the air, sending one of the crew flying while at the same time it rounded on the remaining two. With its massive jaws open the creature leapt forwards was pinned one of the remaining two in its mouth. Biting down, Cathy knew what was coming and clamped her eyes shut as a piercing scream carried in the air before it abruptly stopped.

Knowing what had happened, Cathy opened her eyes and saw the enormous creature swallowing what remained of the dead crewmate. Turning away, Cathy saw that the Croinsop had once again got Flash pinned against the wall as the agile feline fought to get himself free.

Not wanting to pay any more attention to the evil creature, Cathy launched herself up and sprinted across to help Flash. With its back to her, the Croinsop was caught by surprise as Cathy jumped onto its back and buried the blunt sword down into a narrow gap between its armoured back and neck.

The blade sank deep, and the Croinsop screamed in pain as Cathy dropped down and ran around to assist Flash. Consumed by the searing pain and the wedge sword, the Croinsop dropped its weapons and flailed around, desperately trying to pull the sword free that Cathy had left in place.

'Come on, we need to run.' Cathy hissed as she helped Flash to his feet.

'I cannot go.' Flash wheezed as he dropped to one knee.

'Why, what's wrong?'

As Cathy asked, she saw the answer. In the time she had been distracted by everything else, the Croinsop had managed to drive one of its axes across the upper part of Flash's leg. While the blade had not severed his leg, it was barely hanging on. In his haste, Flash had tied his belt around the gaping wound, but already his fur was matted with dirt and blood.

'Let me help.' Cathy begged, as she helped him to sit against the arena wall.

'You must save yourself, I'm done for.'

'No.' Cathy protested as she pulled the belt tighter to stop the bleeding.

As she fastened the buckle, Flash placed his paw on her hand and stopped her. Not daring to look up, Cathy felt the tears well in her eyes as Flash lifted her chin and forced her to look at him.

'You should not have been here.' Flash coughed. 'The crew of the Lady Chance have let you down, it was our job to protect you.'

'You're wrong. It should have been me protecting you, like my brothers did.'

Flash tapped his paw on the Aralcym that Cathy still gripped in her hand.

'You underestimate yourself, Cathy Scott. I believe in you, my crew believe in you and I know you have it in you.' Flash's eyes were heavy as he struggled to keep them open. 'I think I'll take a nap now.'

'Please, don't leave me.'

'I'm not going anywhere, I'll be back on the Lady Chance in no time.'

As a chilling roar filled the arena, Cathy turned away from Flash as his paw slipped from the top of her hand. Looking out across the sand, Cathy realised she was the only one left and her attention fell to the sickly creature as it finished devouring another of the dead crew from the arena floor.

Rising to her feet, Cathy recovered one of the axes left by the Croinsop and turned to face the creature. As she prepared to fight, the crowd fell silent and the Dark Queen's voice carried in the air.

'As impressed as I am, Cathy Scott, your time has come.' Her voice echoed all around. 'I offer you one final chance to surrender to me and bow to my will or face your end at the hands of my Argyle.'

In response, the fearsome black creature dropped to sit on its hind legs and turned its sleek face towards the Dark Queen in the pulvinus.

'No.' Cathy replied, tightening her grip on the Aralcym and axe handle. 'I'm not going to help you, so you might as well tell them to kill me.'

'I must say, I am disappointed.' The Dark Queen sighed as she sat down in her ornate throne. 'Your answer is not unexpected.'

Raising her hand into the air, she clenched her fist and dropped it to her side. In response, the Argyle rose onto all fours and turned its head to face Cathy. Cathy felt her heart skip a beat as the Argyle exposed its maw of razor-sharp teeth and curled its lip into an evil snarl.

Cathy knew this was the end.

CHAPTER TWENTY

FACING THE ARGYLE

The crowd remained silent as the remaining Croinsop and gargoyles left the arena. Cathy was not as confident as she had tried to make herself sound as she watched the arena floor empty, leaving only her and the enormous Argyle on the sand.

Even at a distance across the arena, she could see how big the creature was. All smooth black armoured skin and spikes, the Argyle was a cross between all the nightmarish monsters she could think of, dragons, dinosaurs, werewolves and more. It was as if whatever had birthed it had taken the most dangerous elements of each monster and moulded them into this.

Having given the command, the body-language of the Argyle had changed. It now stalked slowly on the far side of the arena, sniffing the air as if tasting Cathy's fear. Moving like a stalking panther, the Argyle moved with purpose as it circled around Cathy, hugging itself close to the outer walls. Despite its movement and the Dark Queen's announcement, the crowd remained eerily quiet.

The air was charged and electric, Cathy could feel hundreds of eyes watching as she waited for the

Argyle to attack. Not taking her eyes off the magnificent creature, it moved past Flash who Cathy was pretty sure was dead. As the swooshing tail whipped past Flash's head, Cathy was convinced she saw his eyelids flutter and the simple sign of life gave her hope.

Knowing the Argyle was toying with her, stalking its prey without concern, she waited for the inevitable attack. Knowing she could never best the Argyle if she attacked first, all she could do was wait.

Taking a step back, her feet kicked something on the ground and Cathy dared to look down. Half buried in the sand, Cathy gasped as she recognised the mask from the alleyway window at Painted Point, the one the Croinsop had given her when she had hidden on the Lady Chance. Remembering the Croinsop in the alley that had offered to hide her aboard the Lady Chance, it seemed impossible that the mask was here. Lifting the warrior mask from the ground, she dusted off the sand.

Still keeping the stalking Argyle in her peripheral vision, Cathy turned the mask over and admired the simple decoration on the bone-white mask. A solid black line divided the mask in half from top to bottom while two pairs of black lines had been painted above the empty eyeholes.

Lifting her attention to the Argyle, Cathy caught sight of Flash once again, this time with a Croinsop towering over him. As she was about to shout out in protest, Cathy watched as the Croinsop hoisted Flash to his feet and began dragging him to a narrow opening a little further along the wall.

With the Argyle motionless, watching Cathy's every move through its four shimmering eyes, Cathy saw the

Croinsop help Flash through the opening. Resting his blooded paw on the stone, Flash turned to look at Cathy through the legs of the mighty beast. With all his effort, his face and fur drained from his injury, Flash motioned for Cathy to put on the mask.

'That's ridiculous.' Cathy huffed, but nonetheless, did as Flash instructed.

Taking hold of the band, Cathy lifted the mask over her face and tucked the elastic material beneath her hair. Smoothing the mask to her face, it took a few seconds to adjust to the tightness of the mask, but when she opened her eyes, she saw the world completely differently.

Peering through the once hollow eyes, Cathy was unaware that they now glowed a brilliant pale blue. Peering through the prism lenses, Cathy now saw the world in a curiously pale light. As she turned her attention to the Argyle, she saw its movements seemed to leave a trail of pale light in its wake, as if the mask was somehow allowing her to see more of the world than before.

As Cathy was about to remove the mask, the Argyle flinched enough to send a ripple of light from its front legs and lunged forward to attack. With no other choice, Cathy gripped the axe in her hand and prepared to fight.

It did not take long for Cathy to realise how dangerous the Argyle was. For every attack it made with its powerful jaws, it met that attack with a swing of its spiked tail. Every time Cathy thought she had defended herself, she would sense the movement of the tail in time to see the spike silver bones hurtling through the air towards her.

Ducking and diving, Cathy soon found it hard to breathe in the tight mask as the Argyle relentlessly bore down on her. As she swung the axe out in an attempt to block the enormous clawed paw smashing into her, she felt a swell of pride as the Argyle yelped and leapt back.

The blade of the axe was tainted with blood as the Argyle inspected a jagged wound across the pad of its paw. Curling its lips, the creature released a terrifying snarl that thundered in the air. Holding her composure, Cathy fought to calm her racing brain as she tried to think about how she could survive.

Casting aside the sudden pain, the Argyle propelled itself into the air and swept its tail up and around at Cathy. With nowhere to turn, all Cathy could do was raise the axe to protect herself, but it was no use. Avoiding the spiked bones, Cathy felt the full force of the attack as the muscular tail slammed into the axe-handle, sending her hurtling through the air.

Cathy crashed to the ground and was sent rolling head over feet until she came to a stop facing up to the stormy sky. Fighting to refill her lungs, her hands were empty as the shattered axe and Aralcym had tumbled to the ground mid-flight. Shaking away the sea of stars in her vision, Cathy looked around and saw the broken handle and snapped blade of the axe on the ground between her and the Argyle, the Aralcym on the other hand had come to rest by the side of her head.

Snatching the Aralcym, Cathy rose to her knees as she fought to catch her breath. Staring at the open mouths on either end of the stone carvings, Cathy closed her eyes and willed the Eternal Flame to answer.

Not daring to open her eyes, Cathy could hear the sounds of the Argyle as it once again stalked its prey at a distance. Clamping her eyes shut behind the mask, Cathy fought to put herself on the crossbeams of the Lady Chance.

It was not easy. Every snarling breath of the Argyle felt dangerously close, but she knew she needed to concentrate. Shutting out every distraction, Cathy calmed her mind and gripped the Aralcym tighter than she ever had before.

Knowing this was her only chance of survival, Cathy yelped as she felt the warmth once again in her palm. Unlike before, the warmth grew until it felt as if her skin would blister. Fighting against the heat and pain, Cathy opened her eyes and looked on in disbelief.

Fire poured from the open mouths on either end of the Aralcym. Although it was an achievement, the fire was not under her control and simply poured out to the ground at her feet. Sensing her confusion, the Argyle leapt forward and attacked again.

With little option, Cathy raised the Aralcym into the air and sent the spewing flames out in the direction of the Argyle. The fire glanced off the creature's smooth exterior and it appeared to do nothing to stop its attack.

Dropping to the ground, Cathy held the Aralcym above her and watched as the spewing fire formed a shield around her. Landing with its front feet on either side of her, Cathy watched as the Argyle chomped and bit at the domed shield.

The flaming shield was the only thing protecting her from certain death. With each attack, more of the flowing fire dripped down onto Cathy's mask, but she remained firm. Pinned in position, the Argyle lifted its uninjured paw and slammed it down on top of the flaming shield.

Feeling herself pressed into the ground with the immense weight of the creature, Cathy struggled to keep the Aralcym handle raised above her and felt it pressed towards her body. Trapped and pinned, there was nothing she could do as sweat stung her eyes.

As the Argyle hammered down on the shield of fire, Cathy knew she couldn't hold it for much longer. With each blow, her arms compressed lower to her chest until the shield was held only inches from her face. Desperate and trapped, Cathy made one last-ditch attempt to free herself from beneath the Argyle.

As the Argyle raised its paw to strike again, Cathy released her control on the Aralcym and willed the flame to listen to her. At first nothing happened and as the Argyle crushed down on her again, she wasn't sure she had it in her like her brothers.

The thought of Timothy wielding his Nosym with ease filled her with grim determination.

'I want you to be a sword.' She screamed at the top of her lungs as the Argyle lifted its paw again.

Her cry of desperation echoed in the air as the shield evaporated and was miraculously replaced with a flaming blade that cut through the flesh of the Argyle's lower leg as it moved to crush Cathy. The shrill cry of pain carried in the air as Cathy drove the flaming sword up and over her head, glancing off the Argyle's other leg.

Recoiling from the sudden turn of events, the Argyle scurried away with its injured leg held high in the air. Recoiling from the searing pain, the Argyle snarled, but kept its distance as Cathy rose to her feet. Still gripping in the flaming sword, she turned to look at the Dark Queen, who was now standing at the edge of her viewing area.

'Seize her.' The Dark Queen commanded and in an instant all the small doors opened in the arena wall.

Reinvigorated by the sudden turn of events, Cathy was not ready to surrender. Dropping low, she recalled everything Sky had taught her and prepared to fight. The first Croinsop to reach Cathy were dealt with easily as Cathy allowed the view through the mask to give her an idea where to attack. Seeing the movements of her attackers like ripples in water, it felt as if she could almost predict where they were moving.

Thrusting and jabbing, Cathy managed to dispatch a dozen of the guards before the Argyle had regained its senses. Barrelling through the Croinsop and gargoyles, the Argyle screamed towards Cathy, but she was ready.

Listening to her senses, trusting her sudden confidence, Cathy launched into the air as the Argyle attacked. She had seen her brothers and mother fight like this, somehow trusting themselves to the power the Eternal Flame gave them, and now she could understand it herself. Swelling with pride, Cathy rotated in the air and, in one fell swoop, severed the Argyle's head from its body.

As the lifeless corpse of the enormous monster crashed to the ground, Cathy landed on top of its torso and glared across at the Dark Queen.

Before she could say a word a bolt of lightning burst from the sky and in a heartbeat Cathy's body was filled with pain. Unable to move her muscles spasmed as the electricity coursed through her. Feeling herself hoisted into the air, Cathy was powerless to resist as two of the three columns rose from the floor. Moved by the Dark Queen's power, Cathy was hoisted between the two pillars and at last, the pain and lightning stopped.

Cathy found herself bound to the two pillars, her arms and legs help in place by crackling chains of electricity. Unable to pull herself free, Cathy watched as the Dark Queen sauntered across the arena floor to stand in front of her.

'I knew you would help me.' The Dark Queen mocked as she stroked the back of her hand against Cathy's youthful cheek. 'I remember being your age, I had already proven myself in battle.'

'I'll never help you.' Cathy growled through gritted teeth.

'Oh, Cathy Scott You already have.'

Cathy followed the Dark Queen's gaze as she looked towards the spiked spires of the arena. A ring of fire burned between each of the eight points and Cathy knew it had been the fire she had created that was doing it.

'You've given me the one thing I could never have to complete the ritual.' The Dark Queen's sinister laugh filled Cathy's ears as she felt her surge of pride evaporate in an instant. 'I could never control the Eternal Flame but you, you have done that for me.'

Cathy had survived the arena but at what cost?

CHAPTER TWENTY-ONE

CATHY'S FALL

Cathy was left alone as the stadium emptied. Still restrained, tied to the two columns, there was enough slack in the sizzling electrical restraints so she could sit down. Sitting cross-legged on the sandy floor, she watched as the array of bodies were removed from the arena.

Not daring to count the number of the Lady Chance's crew that had fallen to the Dark Queen's warriors, she scuffed the floor with her feet to stay distracted. Once everyone was gone, there was nothing but the sound of sizzling electricity that acted as her chains and a curious twinkling sound that came from the jagged ring of fire high above.

Looking up towards the sky, Cathy couldn't make sense of what she was seeing. Each spire of the vast arena shimmered in the sunlight as the tendrils of flame connected each of the eight spires. Even though Cathy was unsure what was happening, it didn't take a genius to understand.

Although she couldn't make out the source of the light atop the spires, she suspected they were the Gonks-Venit that Nasser and Sky had spoken of. If that were the case, Cathy suspected the connecting fire she had created was somehow activating them.

'Beautiful, isn't it?' The Dark Queen's voice was calm as she moved across the arena towards her.

Cathy chose not to acknowledge the Dark Queen, choosing instead to toy with the piles of stand she had made on the floor in front of her. Her shadow covered Cathy as she moved around to stand in front of her.

'You should be proud of what you've done.' The Dark Queen dropped to her haunches and grabbed Cathy's chin, forcing her to look at her. 'Without you, this wouldn't have been possible.'

The Dark Queen raised Cathy's attention back to the shimmering lights and connecting flame. Not wanting to look, Cathy pulled her face from the Queen's grip and glared at her. Once again, Cathy could only admire her regal prowess and the impressive armoured dress she wore.

'Why should I be proud? You tricked me into doing it.'

'Oh my sweet girl, I helped you realise your true potential.'

Somehow, the Queen was offended by Cathy's rebuke as she rose to her feet. Cathy could sense the Dark Queen's desire to have Cathy understand her reasoning. The way she spoke, the way she acted, it told Cathy she longed to see her as something more than a mere prisoner or tool to use. It felt almost motherly.

'Sky was showing me, you didn't help me at all.'

'Didn't I?' The Dark Queen smirked as she admired the dancing fire. 'Were you able to conjure the Eternal Flame the way you did here when you were with him?'

'Well, no.'

'I gave you the motivation to reach your full potential, not treat you like a child and inch you along the path.'

'You almost killed me.' Cathy snapped as she rose to her feet. 'You were more than happy to let me die at the hands of your pet monster.'

'The Argyle?' Once again, the Queen laughed as she turned her attention back to Cathy. 'My pet was nothing more than another test for you. I would not have let you fall to it.'

Cathy followed the Dark Queen's gaze to the back of the arena and her heart sank as she saw the corpse of the enormous monster, its carcass hidden beneath a fluttering sheet of material.

'I always knew you were strong enough to defeat it.'

'How could you be so sure?'

'I see it in you, Cathy. Where Sky would see you swim in your own self-doubt, haven't I shown you how you can push beyond that and realise your full potential?'

'I preferred Sky's way.'

The Dark Queen was about to reply when they were interrupted by Dux's arrival. Flying towards them, the Ecilop came to hover in front of the Dark Queen with his back to Cathy.

'My Queen,' Dux panted as he caught his breath. 'The Argyle is ready for you.'

'I killed it.' Cathy declared as Dux rounded to face her.

'You defeated one of them, yes.' Dux snapped, dismissing Cathy's curious look.

'I'll be with you in a few moments.' The Dark Queen replied. 'Now, leave us alone.'

On the Queen's command, Dux flew past Cathy and offered her a distasteful look. As the Ecilop flew by her head, Cathy felt his wings whip past her cheek. There was something about Dux she did not like, the time she had spent in Poc told her that Dux was a far cry from the Ecilop that lived there. As she watched him flying away she felt no warmth towards him and she could not understand how he could have become that way.

'What do you do to people?'

'What do you mean?'

'You take innocent things, like Dux, and make them work for you. He's an Ecilop, they're lovely and yet you have him here killing people and fighting each other.'

'He's here by choice.' The Dark Queen snapped, her frustration showing through. 'My servants know that I am the rightful heir to all of this.'

'Rightful heir to what?'

'Mielikuvitus, your world, all of it.'

'Says who?'

In a heartbeat, the Dark Queen was on Cathy and lowered her face until their noses were almost touching. Her eyes burned with anger and this close, Cathy could see the tiny sparks of electricity moving between the strands of blue hair on her head.

'You have no idea who I am, do you?'

'You've already told me.' Cathy's flippant answer clearly riled the Dark Queen. 'You're the Dark Queen, rightful heir to a world that doesn't need you. I may only be eleven but I can see the truth.'

'What would that be?'

'You're a lost girl, a bit like me, filled with doubt and wanting to prove to everyone you can be something.'

Cathy's defiance caught the Queen by surprise. Taking a moment to find her answer, she could not help but admire Cathy's tenacity.

'My father was of this world, my mother was not.' The Dark Queen began as she toyed with the electrical restraints holding Cathy in place. 'My mother came here to serve a master who had no right to hold the power he did.'

'Was that the old woman at the house?'

'You're a perceptive girl.' She mused as she traced her slender fingers through the dancing electricity. 'As you know, time passes differently between our worlds. When you were last here, your brother met my mother.'

'When?'

'She served the Dark Entity.'

'Dr Live?' Cathy gasped. 'Tim told me all about her, but how can she be your mum?'

'She fled when the Entity fell for the first time but fought alongside it when your parents and brothers ventured into the Neverending Caves.'

'So your dad is the Dark Entity?'

The sudden outburst of laughter caught Cathy by surprise.

'The essence of the Dark Entity was nothing more than that, tendrils of evil personified in a weak form of your father's fallen Ecilop.'

'So who is he?'

'My father was a creature of this world who, much like the Dark Entity, failed to achieve his full potential. A creature who turned from true power despite everything. My mother had a way of finding herself in service of such people.' The Dark Queen's resentment of her father was clear in her tone of voice.

Stalking away, Cathy's questioning had obviously upset the Dark Queen. Brimming with anger, Cathy watched her blue hair ripple with electricity. Taking a moment to compose herself, Cathy felt unsure of herself for a moment and was unsure how the Dark Queen would react. As the slender woman turned to face her, there was an unfamiliar look on her face, something that chilled Cathy to the core.

'Who was he?'

'Isn't it obvious?' The Dark Queen teased.

'No.'

'Then it will remain a mystery to you.'

The Dark Queen stormed past Cathy without a second glance. The change in her composure caught Cathy by surprise as the Queen stalked away towards the covered corpse of the Argyle.

'What are you going to do?'

'Achieve what no other has.' The Dark Queen replied without turning back. 'Rise to power and rule both worlds as I was destined to do.'

'Our worlds aren't supposed to be together, that's why there are mirrors.'

'Only because they are afraid of completing the process, because they know your world will fall to ours.'

'Sky said both would be destroyed.'

'Yes.' The Dark Queen boomed as she reached the far end of the arena. 'And in its wake a new world, my world, will be born.'

Utterly dismayed, Cathy dropped to her knees and knew she had been defeated. Although the Queen had shown some small amount of softness, it had quickly evaporated when Cathy had pressed her. There was something about her avoidance of Cathy's questions about her father, but Cathy realised it meant nothing now.

Defeated, Cathy looked around at the arena and then a thought crossed her mind. Dusting her hands of sand, Cathy scanned the floor for any sign of her Aralcym. In the moments after she had defeated the Argyle, she remembered dropping it, but did not know where it had fallen. The fact the Dark Queen had not shown it to her told Cathy it was somewhere in the arena.

At first Cathy could see no sign of the carved heads and bound handle on the ground. Looking further afield than where she stood, Cathy caught sight of something shimmering in the sunlight. Standing, Cathy narrowed her eyes and recognised the carved head half-buried in the sand almost a quarter of the way across the arena floor, away from her.

The shimmering stone was mocking her as it glinted in the sunlight. The Aralcym could have been on the beach with her family and still be as useful to her as it was now. Seeing the weapon only told reminded her how powerless she was. Bound and restrained between the two columns, she could not free herself from the crackling bonds. Whatever dark magic the Queen had used was unbreakable by Cathy.

There was nothing she could do to free herself, nothing she could to stop the Dark Queen. Although she had no idea how they would now cross the worlds, Cathy knew the time was coming.

As if in answer to her unspoken questions, the air was filled with trumpets and the sound of marching feet. Looking behind her, Cathy watched as the oversized gates to the arena opened and Cathy felt her stomach turn at the sight that greeted her.

Scores of armour-clad soldiers, Croinsop and gargoyle alike, marched behind the Dark Queen who now sat astride another Argyle. If it were even possible, the creature beneath the Dark Queen was even bigger than the one Cathy had faced in the arena. The Argyle sported a silver headpiece of armour and a painted red stripe along the length of its body.

The soldiers held at the gates as the Dark Queen guided the Argyle towards Cathy. Staring up at the enormous creature, Cathy felt a sudden surge of fear as she felt the vibrations in the ground with each step the creature took. As the Dark Queen brought the Argyle to a stop, Cathy could feel its hot breath cascade over her.

Craning her neck to look up at the Argyle, Cathy waited for the Queen to speak.

'This should show you my strength and also my lenience. You killed her baby and yet, at my command, she doesn't take her revenge.'

Cathy could feel the eyes of the Argyle boring into her from behind the armoured headpiece.

'Why not let it?'

'Because I want you to see what you created.' The Dark Queen answered as she pointed towards the tendrils of flame. 'And who knows, when this is over, perhaps you will realise your power and take your place beside me.'

'I won't.'

'We shall see.'

Sending a bolt of lightning up into the sky, Cathy watched as it collided with the flame connecting the shimmering stones and the sky itself disappeared. The area inside the octagon of connected spires went black and appeared at first as a shimmering mist.

'Watch as I create the one true portal.' The Queen declared as the mist swirled and moved.

Hypnotised by the swirling smoke, Cathy watched as the octagon changed shape and for a moment, the surface became a sheet of sheer glass. Reflecting the view of the of the arena floor, Cathy could see herself in the mirror the Dark Queen had created.

'What are you going to do?'

'I'm going to claim your world.'

As the Dark Queen answered, a circle of orange light appeared in the mirror's centre and expanded outwards. Filled with a pearlescent smoke, Cathy knew this was the pathway between the two worlds.

She had failed as she realised the Dark Queen had now connected the two worlds.

CHAPTER TWENTY-TWO

DEFEATED

Having been saved from the arena floor by one of the Croinsop, Flash sat in a dark room, fighting to stay awake. The pain in his leg was almost unbearable and although Cathy had helped stem the bleeding, he knew he was going to lose his leg.

'You fought valiantly.' His rescuer announced as he shuffled across the room.

'Not well enough though.' Flash feigned a smile as he looked up at the ceiling.

'You're going to lose that, you know right?'

'It's not a surprise.'

'I can fix it.'

The Croinsop from the alley stepped into view holding a roll of bandage and a large dagger in his other hand. For a moment Flash looked at the jagged blade and in response only offered a curt nod.

'Get on with it.' Flash sighed and closed his eyes.

It was done in a heartbeat, and despite the sudden surge of pain, Flash felt nothing once the task was done. Lowering his gaze to the Croinsop, it pleased him the creature had removed the leg out of sight.

'Drink this.' The Croinsop thrust a small vial into Flash's shaking hands.

'What is it?'

'Something my people use in battle.' The Croinsop answered as he once again disappeared into the darker shadows on the far side of the room. 'It will sting for a moment, but your wound will heal. We call it Night Venom.'

'Sounds delightful.' Flash groaned as he sniffed the dark liquid. 'Don't you have it in a nicer flavour?'

'Just drink.'

The Croinsop busied himself in the shadows as Flash covered his nose and gulped down the contents of the vial. It was thick and disgusting, flowing down his throat like treacle. Coughing against the taste, he dropped the vial on the floor and took a long breath in.

The wound at his leg felt no different, at first, until a sudden pain erupted like nothing he had ever felt before. Doing all he could to fight against screaming, Flash writhed on the floor as the Croinsop watched from the shadows. The jagged wound smouldered as the flesh knitted together, leaving a stump that looked to be made of the same dark substance as the Croinsop's outer shell.

'That hurt!' Flash sighed as the pain subsided and he looked up at the Croinsop towering over him. 'Why would you help me?'

'I come from Painted Point, it was my supplies that filled your hold before leaving for the Chigem Mines.'

'But why are you here?'

'I was asked to follow in the shadows by Sky, to make sure you were not followed or accosted on your journey.'

'You didn't do a wonderful job of that.'

The Croinsop dropped his gaze, knowing that Flash was right.

'I admit I was absent when the Dark Queen attacked you, I thought you were safe and sought an audience with Sky.'

'What happened to my ship?'

'The Dark Queen left nothing afloat of your armada.' The Croinsop could not meet Flash's gaze. 'I'm afraid your Lady chance now sits at the bottom of Rainbow River.'

Sky's bright eyes filled with tears. Not only had he lost his crew but his home, his ship, his salvation had been taken from him. The Dark Queen had destroyed everything he held dear to him.

'Sky, where is he now?' Flash asked as he sat up. 'Does he know we are here? Is he coming?'

'They retook the Chigem Mines, and it was him who sent me here to aid Cathy and your crew escape the arena.'

The mention of his crew sent another wave of sadness through Flash. Despite surviving the battle in the arena, Flash had seen many of his friends fall. To him, his crew were his family, and even the memory of them filled him with sorrow.

'Is he here, with you?'

'Sky remained behind, tending to the wounded left alive by the Dark Queen.'

'How many were there, how many survived the attack?'

'Enough.' The answer told Flash there had been very few left behind alive after the ambush.

Allowing Flash a moment, the Croinsop busied himself once again in the shadows before returning to stand in front of Flash. The Croinsop held a wooden stump in his hand and offered it out to Flash, who eyed it with curiosity.

'I am not some pirate.' Flash scoffed as he pushed away the offering.

'How do you suppose to rescue Miss Scott if all you can do is hop on one leg?' The Croinsop dropped the peg leg to the floor at Flash's foot.

Knowing the Croinsop was right, Flash scooped up the wooden leg. Admiring the craftsmanship, he realised the length was adjustable and was already fitted with a leather brace to attach around his waist.

'You just happen to carry one of these around with you?'

'On the contrary, I know where they are kept in the Dark Queen's Arena.'

'How would you know that?'

'Many years ago I was the medicus here. Before the great battle, I was one of many who would care for the dying and wounded of battle. This arena was once the pride of the Croinsop, before the Dark Queen claimed it as her own.'

'I thought you were on our side.'

'I am.' The Croinsop sighed. The weight of his past was heavy. 'I was born for war, forced to fight until I realised my own fate lay away from all of this. That's when I found my way to Painted Point and made a life away from battle and war.'

'Is that why Sky sent you, because you know this place?'

'Yes.'

'Then I'm glad he sent you.' Flash declared as he fastened the buckles around his waist and used the wall to stand up. 'Whatever your name is, I owe you my life. That is something I will not forget.'

'You owe me nothing. I am atoning for my sins in service to the Dark Entity when I was in my youth.'

'I choose what I owe and to whom!' Flash interrupted the Croinsop's melancholy reply. 'Now, what do you say we find Cathy and escape this place?'

'It will not be that simple.'

'What do you mean?'

'The ritual has already begun. I heard the call to order and the sound of marching. The Dark Queen has succeeded in activating the Gonks-Venit and opened the portal between our world and Cathy Scott's.'

Adjusting the length of the wooden leg, Flash tested his weight on it and felt how unstable he suddenly was. Doing his best to stay upright, Flash felt unbalanced as he stepped away from the wall.

'Is there anything we can do?'

'To stop the crossing? No.' The Croinsop moved to open a door on the far side of the room. 'There is hope that we can rescue Cathy Scott and return her to Sky.'

'Then what?'

'We both know the outcome of the two worlds connecting, we know that it is only a matter of time before the worlds collide and everything we know will be reshaped into a new world.'

'Is there nothing we can do?'

'I don't know.'

Sensing the futility in his answer, the Croinsop opened the door and checked they were alone in the labyrinth of corridors beneath the arena. Seeing and hearing nothing, he offered Flash a hand as they emerged from the old medical room and made their way back towards the arena surface.

***

Cathy could do nothing as the Dark Queen ordered two of her guards to remove her from the arena. Still restrained by the binds of crackling electricity, Cathy was removed from between the pillars and watched in horror as the binds wrapped themselves around her body. With barely enough ability to move, she was marched across the sand towards one of the narrow doors in the arena wall.

'When I am done, you will emerge into a new world and find your place within it.'

Trying to find the best reply, Cathy chose to say nothing as she was marched through the open door and plunged into the darkness of the arena interior.

The first thing she noticed was the smell. It was not what she had expected. Having learned about Roman Gladiators at school, she had expected the air to be thick with the smell of death. Instead, the smell that greeted her was somehow sweet and inoffensive. Guided along the dark snaking corridors, the light from her electric binds was enough to allow her to see the walls and floor around her.

'She won't win.' Cathy tried to sound convincing but hearing her own voice echoing around her, she knew she didn't.

'The Dark Queen is the only one to unite the worlds since the beginning. She will succeed.'

Cathy was about to answer when another voice ahead of her stole everyone's attention. Both guards tensed at the sudden declaration from the shadows in front of them.

'Your Queen is a fool.' The voice was familiar, but Cathy could not place it.

Hearing her heart pounding in her ears, Cathy fought to see who had spoken. The slightest of movements in the shadows ahead of her caught her attention, but still she could see nothing.

'Show yourself.' One of the guards growled.

'As you wish.' The voice now came from behind them and all three spun around.

Cathy gasped as the silhouette of a Croinsop appeared in front of them. Stepping into the dancing light of her electrical binds, she immediately recognised him as the Croinsop from Painted Point.

'Who are you and why are you not with the army?'

'Because I saw sense a long time ago.'

Before either of the guards could speak again, the Croinsop attacked. Swiping the same blade he had used on Flash's leg, he disabled both guards with sickening speed and accuracy. As both guards were relinquished of their weapons, Cathy jumped as Flash set about removing the crackling electricity from her wrists and body.

'Flash!'

Moving with great care, Flash slowly unwound the restraints from Cathy's body. More than once, a surge of electricity would spark into his hands in warning, but before long, she was able to step free. Glad to be free of the binds, Cathy wrapped her arms around the battered captain of the Lady Chance and kissed him on the cheek.

'Thank you.'

'We should save celebrations, pass me that.' The Croinsop barked as Flash handed him the electrical binds. 'Help me tie this pair.'

Flash and the Croinsop made short work of securing their prisoners and finding a small room to lock them in. When they returned into the corridor, Cathy took in Flash's appearance and noted the wooden leg. Doing her best not to look afraid or disgusted, she sensed Flash's eyes on her and blushed in the dark corridor.

'Sorry, I didn't mean to stare.'

'It's fine. I've got to get used to it too.' Flash confessed as he tightened the leather around his waist. 'It's all new to me, but I have him to thank for saving me.'

'No thanks are needed.'

'What's your name?' Cathy interrupted, realising she had never had a proper introduction.

'We are not born with names, but when I turned my back on my people, I adopted one.'

'What is it?'

'Galastial Wonereheb, it means I walk alone.'

'Well, Galastial, thank you.'

A sudden crack of thunder rocked the floor and sent plumes of dust and dirt to tumble from the ceiling. Knowing what it meant, Galastial turned and sprinted back towards the door that Cathy had been marched through not moments before.

Following on his heels, Cathy left Flash to hobble along the corridor behind them. As they emerged back into the daylight of the arena, Cathy gasped as she saw the Dark Queen astride the Argyle rising into the air towards the swirling portal. A second crash of thunder rumbled in the air as the Dark Queen was snatched up by some unseen force and disappeared from view.

'It's too late now. Galastial sighed as he ushered Cathy back through the open door and out of sight of the army gathered on the sand.

'What are we going to do?'

'I'm not sure there is anything we can do.'

Flash joined them after a moment, panting from having struggled to find purchase and speed on his wooden leg. As the three of them took in what had happened, a sense of fear and dared hung heavy over them in the darkness of the tunnel. Cathy felt very much like she had failed everyone.

Dejected and upset, Cathy pushed past Flash and moved back along the corridor, wiping the tears from her face.

'Leave her for a moment.' Galastial held Flash's shoulder as he sensed the captain wanting to comfort her. 'She needs a little time alone.'

CHAPTER TWENTY-THREE

ON THE BEACH

Susan had been fast asleep, enjoying the relaxation as the children played on the rocks. Allowing sleep to swallow her, it was a sudden change in temperature that woke her. Opening her eyes, it took a moment to take in why the sun had vanished.

Alone on the beach, the family had found the shelter of the cove alongside the eerie mansion, precariously balanced on the rocks. Scanning around, Susan felt a sudden surge of concern, as she could no longer see the house or even the road behind them.

'Gerard, wake up.'

Shaking the snoring body next to her, her husband groaned as he brushed her hand away.

'Five more minutes.' Gerard huffed as he rolled onto his stomach.

'Gerard, now.'

The worry in Susan's voice snatched him back from his sleep and he sat up to look at her. Wiping the sleep from his eyes, Gerard look up and around and saw the same thick fog that had rolled in from the sea and surrounded the secluded cover.

'What's going on, I thought it was supposed to be nice all day.'

'It was.'

Susan rose to her feet and brushed the sand from her legs. With the sudden sea fog, she felt the chill against her skin as the sun disappeared behind the clouds. Across the sand, she could make out the rocks where Aiden and Timothy had been playing, but saw no sign of Cathy or Evie.

'Boys?' Gerard hollered across the beach as he slipped on a t-shirt over his head. 'Where's your sister?'

Aiden and Timothy dropped from the rocks and sprinted across the beach towards them. As ever, they shared a moment of competition and despite being teenagers, there was still the boyish competitiveness between them.

Arriving first, Timothy skidded to a victorious stop, sending sand splashing over both his parents.

'I win.' Timothy panted as he brushed himself down.

'Only because you're a skinny runt.' Aiden coughed as he jogged the last few steps to join him.

'Boys, shut up for a second.' Susan snapped, her abruptness catching both boys by surprise. 'Where's your sister?'

'I don't know.' Aiden answered, as he looked back at the foggy rocks.

'Neither do I.' Timothy agreed. 'What about you, Aleobe?'

'She was on the rocks before the fog rolled in. I saw her near the old house.'

Aleobe remained unseen away from Mielikuvitus but now, since the family had returned from facing the Dark Entity, the whole family could now hear him. His playful and cheerful voice was now at odds with the seriousness of Susan's concern.

'Can you have a look if you can see her, Aleobe?' Gerard snapped as he read what Susan was thinking.

'I'll go.' Aiden offered but was stopped from moving as his father grabbed his shoulder.

'What's wrong?'

As if to answer Aiden's question, a sudden rumble of thunder brought all of their attention towards the sea and the rocks. Through the pale fog, a darker patch suddenly appeared and, if it was possible, they all felt the air grow even colder.

'Get your things.' Susan reached for the bag on the sand.

'Where are we going?' Timothy pressed as he reached for his rucksack.

'Nowhere.' His dad replied and reached into Susan's bag. 'Get ready.'

'You mean?'

'Yes.'

Gerard withdraw the bound handle of his Nekorb as Susan withdrew her Efiwym. Before either of the boys could speak, they watched as their parents called the Eternal Flame from the open maws of the carved figures and turned their attention to the dark patch of cloud as it grew larger.

'I thought we weren't supposed to use them here?'

'Get them.' Susan snapped as the dark cloud inched closer.

As both boys withdrew their weapons from the beach bag, they turned to look as bolts of lightning crackled and snapped from the corona of darkness as it reached the edge of the sand. Swirling behind the pale fog, the dark cloud swirled until the fog was called towards it and a portal appeared above the beach. All four sets of eyes watched in disbelief and horror as the swirling darkness grew wider and a figure emerged from it.

The first thing to pass between the two worlds was the armoured face of the Argyle. Despite the hidden sun, the metal helmet glinted in the light as the Dark Queen's ride passed through the portal and onto the beach.

Inch by inch, the enormous monster stalked towards them until the Dark Queen finally emerged astride the enormous beast. The size of the Argyle almost filled the beach as it dragged its tail through the portal and dropped to its haunches to allow the Dark Queen to climb down to the sand.

'It's nice to see some of you are in control of your powers.'

The Dark Queen's sinister tone was obvious as she sauntered across the sand towards them. Dressed in the same armoured dress, she took a moment for her arrival to sink in to the astounded family. Although Susan and Gerard had called forth their flames, they remained poised and ready to strike as the Dark Queen moved towards them.

'I am unarmed, as you can see.' She offered both hands out by her side. 'I offer you no threat.'

'I can only imagine why you decided to ride in on that thing then, a show of force perhaps?' Gerard snarled as she forged the Eternal Flame into a double-bladed sword.

'I don't need an Argyle to show my power and position.'

'And who exactly are you?' Timothy interrupted as he looked the Dark Queen up and down.

'My dear Timothy Scott, your sister certainly admires your skills.'

'Where is she?' Susan snapped and stepped in front of her family, simmering with anger. 'Where is my daughter?'

'She's safe.'

'Give her back to me.' Susan levelled her flaming axe towards the Dark Queen. 'I won't ask again.'

'My dear Susan, you and your family offer me no threat. Not now I have fulfilled the prophecy and crossed the void between our worlds.'

'For what reason?' Gerard asked as he moved to Susan's side.

'To create a world fit for a Queen. Fit for me.'

'You still haven't told us who you are.' Aiden quizzed as he birthed the Eternal Flame from his Nodwons.

'I am the Dark Queen of the Forgottenlands, born from both sides of the mirror, and destined to combine our worlds.'

'Sounds like a load of rubbish to me.' Aiden smirked as he saw the irritation on the slender Queen's pale face.

'How dare you?'

Bubbling with frustration, the Dark Queen raised her hand and formed a ball of lightning between her fingers and allowed it to hover above her palm. It was more a display of power than anything else as she toyed with the orb of electricity for a moment before speaking again.

'Your daughter helped me to forge the channel between our worlds.' The Dark Queen floated the orb in the air for a moment. 'You should be very proud of her.'

Susan tensed at the mention of Cathy. Despite the Dark Queen's declaration that Cathy had assisted her, she knew her daughter wouldn't have done anything of the sort. Keeping the flaming axe directed towards the Dark Queen, Susan chose her words carefully.

'My daughter wouldn't help someone intent on taking a world that doesn't belong to them. I will ask you one more time, where is my daughter?'

'She's safe, more than I can say for you if you don't move aside.'

'Why would we do that?'

'Because I am the Dark Queen, it is my birthright to unite our worlds and take my place on a united throne.'

'Our world doesn't work like that.' Timothy protested.

The Dark Queen directed all her attention to Timothy. His unruly red hair enhanced the brightness of his eyes as he glared at her. Despite her presence and prowess, Timothy held her gaze as she bent closer, as if to whisper only to him.

'Your world is no longer what you know it to be. Your world will become mine and it will be as I make it. This will be my design.'

'Not if I have anything to do with it.' Gerard interrupted and swept the flaming blades up towards the Dark Queen's head. 'Boys!'

Knowing what needed to be done, the family attacked in unison.

Surprised by the sudden attack, the Dark Queen moved in time to see the flaming blade swipe through the air where her head had been. Releasing the orb of electricity from her hand, she directed the bolts of lightning out towards Susan and Gerard to give her enough time to escape.

Spinning around, the Dark Queen created two swords of crackling electricity and prepared herself for battle. Although she had crossed the void between the worlds alone, she had done so knowing she would have to face the Partum Spiritus. What she had not explained to Cathy's family was the fact that only she could cross through the portal until she had claimed victory.

The Dark Queen's prophecy was one of isolation, one where her victory would cement her power and allow the convergence to be complete. Without the support of her army, she had prepared for this moment for as long as she could remember. The arena she had forced Cathy to fight in had been her training ground. Years of tutelage at the hands of Mielikuvitus' greatest warriors had prepared her to fight not one, but four Partum Spiritus.

'Take care of the monster.' Susan yelled to the boys as Gerard and her set about protecting their children from the Dark Queen.

Gerard and Susan split either side of the Queen and set about their attacks. To their dismay, they found her to be a formidable adversary as she easily blocked and parried each of their attacks. Armed only with the crackling blades of electricity, she ducked and dodged as each of them thrust with the Eternal Flame.

'Your skills have faded with time away.' The Dark Queen mocked as she once again cast Gerard's attack aside. 'Where you have rested, I have trained for this moment.'

The Dark Queen took advantage of her distraction and brought the tip of her sword scraping across Gerard's chest. As his muscles reacted to the sudden flow of electricity through them, he felt the wind ripped from his lungs and lost all control over his Nekorb. Unable to move, Gerard crashed to the sand as the fire retracted into the open stone mouths on either end of his weapon.

'Gerard.'

'Watch out.' He wheezed as the Dark Queen directed her attention towards Susan.

Susan was too busy with the Dark Queen to see if Timothy and Aiden had made it to the enormous Argyle that sat in front of the swirling portal. The Dark Queen was without a doubt far more skilled than she was. Fighting with all her strength to manipulate the Eternal Flame, Susan knew she was already at a disadvantage, fighting away from Mielikuvitus.

She had only ever birthed the Eternal Flame in our world twice before, and each time the effort had felt much greater than it did on the other side of the mirror. Now, fighting to hold back the relentless attacks of the Dark Queen, she could already feel her mind struggling to keep a grasp on its connection with the Efiwym in her hand.

'You fight only to delay the future.' The Dark Queen snarled as she launched herself into the air and over Susan's head.

Despite wearing the flowing armoured dress, the fabric was designed in such a way to give the Queen freedom to move with ease. Launching herself up and over Susan's head allowed her the chance to drive the crackling sword down towards her opponent. Quick to respond, Susan cast aside the attack and felt a sting of pain as the tip brushed close to her face and she felt the fingers of sparking electricity claw at her skin.

As the Dark Queen landed on the sand, she made a swift move that swept Susan's legs from beneath her, sending her crashing to the ground. Crashing down to land by Gerard's side, the world was upside down and she caught a glimpse of Timothy and Aiden as they fought against the gargantuan Argyle in front of the swirling portal.

Susan was about to speak when she sensed movement out of the corner of her eye as the Dark Queen attacked again.

CHAPTER TWENTY-FOUR

FRIENDS REUNITED

Cathy followed Galastial along the outer edge of the arena. They were afforded glimpses of the vast battleground as they passed the other open doors, but their progress went unnoticed by the Dark Queen's gathered soldiers.

'Where are we going?' Cathy coughed as she fought to keep her breathing under control.

'I was given help to get into the arena.'

'From who?'

'A friend, I would see if they have any idea on what to do next.'

The idea of seeing Sky again filled Cathy with renewed hope. In all the death and destruction she had seen in the arena and aboard the ambushed deck of the Lady Chance, she needed a feeling of hope. The sudden memory of Evie lying on the wooden deck washed over her and she ground to a stop in the corridor.

'What is it?' Flash panted as she hobbled as fast as he could behind her.

'I just remembered something.' Cathy's voice cracked as she fought back the emotion. 'Evie.'

Galastial stopped a short distance ahead of her, his stooped head looking along the remaining length of corridor. Catching sight of the pincer-less Croinsop, Cathy wiped the tears from her face and did her best to cast aside the sadness. Knowing that Sky was waiting for her, she hoped he could find a way for her to make things right.

Not wanting to dwell, Cathy stalked past Galastial and continued along the corridor. Not looking back, she was unaware of Galastial and Flash sharing a hushed conversation before setting off behind her.

'How come I can see you in the daylight?' Cathy quizzed, as she moved along the corridor.

'The arena has an aura around it, some dark magic of the Queen's that makes it impossible for me to hide.' Flash answered, wheezing through the pain.

'It ensures no opponent of her fighters has an unfair advantage.' Galastial continued, but having had her answer, Cathy was focussed on pushing on.

'How much further?' Cathy barked as she stalked along the twisting corridor.

'Two more doors, then out through the one on your left.' Galastial answered from behind her.

'Good.'

Counting off the doors, Cathy found the one she was looking for and reached for the handle. Galastial's hand stopped her from opening the door as she twisted the crooked doorknob. Turning to look at him, she could not hide the revulsion she felt looking so closely at the Croinsop.

'What's wrong?'

'You need to be prepared for what you're about to see.'

'What's happened to Sky? Is he alright?' The concern on her face was impossible to hide as she brushed Galastial's hand away.

'It's not Sky, it's-'

Galastial could not finish his reply before Cathy shoved the door open, and the sunlight beamed in from outside. Shielding her eyes, she allowed them to adjust to the harsh light before stepping out into a large courtyard. The polished black stone reflected the sun in odd prisms of light in every direction, but it was something else that stole her attention.

Against the shimmering black backdrop of polished stone and angular rocks on the far side of the courtyard, there was a figure of brilliant white and blue. Although Cathy's eyes were fighting to focus, she somehow recognised the shape and gasped as the creature came into focus.

With a coat of soft white fur, there was no mistaking the canine face that looked back at her with love and affection. Despite being as big as a horse, it was undeniably Evie that sat patiently in the courtyard's centre, looking at her.

Unable to contain her emotion, Cathy wept as she sprinted the distance between them and wrapped her arms around Evie's massive neck. Struggling to get her hands to meet, Cathy felt her soft fur press against her face as she sobbed into Evie's coat.

'Evie.' She stuttered. 'How? What happened to you? I'm so happy you're alive.'

'Oh, my dear Cathy.' Evie hummed as she nuzzled her oversized nose against Cathy's back. 'I thought I would never see you again.'

'But, what happened to you? Why are you so big?'

'I should let Sky explain.'

On cue, Sky emerged from behind a large, jagged rock to Evie's side. Unlike Evie, Sky looked tired and worn. Cathy noticed the patches of grey in his beard looked larger than she remembered and his normally neat appearance looked more dishevelled and messy. With a subtle hint of a limp, he moved to join Cathy as she released her arms from around Evie's mane.

'I'm glad to see you are unhurt.' Sky nodded as he cast his gaze towards the shimmering portal that was visible over the arena behind her. 'I see the Dark Queen rekindled your connection to the Eternal Flame where I could not.'

'It wasn't like that.' Cathy quickly defended, aware how it must have looked to all of them. 'She tricked me by making me fight in there. I didn't have a choice.'

'Rest easy, Cathy.' Sky soothed as he ruffled her hair. 'I know all too well the devious ways of the Dark Queen. I know you would not have fallen to her side. You were given no choice but to call upon the flame, otherwise we would not be standing her talking now, would we?'

'I guess not.' Cathy still felt she had somehow betrayed him. 'I didn't mean to do it.'

'Cathy, I know you didn't. We all know you didn't, so stop worrying about it.' Sky offered her a somewhat forced smile. 'That said, we need to find a way to fix this, don't you think?'

'Can we? She said it was done.'

'That's where the Dark Queen's obsession has allowed her to see only a single course of action. She cares little for the smaller consequences, as Evie here is proof of.'

'What do you mean?'

'You know that Evie is a Hecate?'

'I've heard it talked about but I don't know what it means.'

'A Hecate is like a seedling, taking one form until such a time as it meets its catalyst. No Hecate is the same. What sparks the change on one may do nothing to another, even if they are of the same bloodline.'

'I don't understand.'

'Think of Evie as a child. Her years would far outlast yours and maybe even mine. While she is happy in her form, her body is always searching for the one thing that will free her. In Evie's case, it was the lightning from the Dark Queen.'

'When that lightning bolt hit me, I felt something I have never felt before.' Evie continued. 'It wasn't pain as you would expect, it was a sense of freedom and power.'

'When a Hecate enters the process of their change, it is much like a caterpillar in your world becoming a butterfly. There needs to be stillness and no interferences as the power is allowed to manifest deep inside.'

As he spoke, Sky rubbed his hand along the length of Evie's side and Cathy watched gob smacked as Evie's fur turned electric blue where he had touched. As he removed his hands, all four of her legs became a mass of spots and veins of blue light, like a mix between the markings of a jaguar and tiger. The same pattern appeared around Evie's eyes and the top of her head, while a pale mist of the same blue wafted from the top of her body.

'When I awoke on the Lady Chance, the Dark Queen had already taken you and I felt like a newborn baby.'

'This is Evie's second life, a newborn Hecate, in her elemental form.'

Cathy admired the beauty and majestic appearance of Evie as she stood in front of her. Despite the shimmering glow and abnormally colossal size, Cathy knew it was still her Evie inside. That had not changed.

'You look amazing.' Cathy eventually offered, as she tentatively reached out a trembling hand to touch the glowing portions of fur.

'It's fine, you can touch me. I promise, I would never hurt you.'

'I know you wouldn't.'

'It might be a problem back home though, don't you think?'

'That is the beauty of it.' Evie declared proudly as she rose onto all fours.

Before her, Cathy watched in stunned silence, as Evie closed her eyes and shrank to her normal size. In a matter of seconds, Evie had gone from being as big as a horse to back to her normal size. Seeing her in a smaller frame was somewhat disappointing, but it was a relief for Cathy to see she could appear normal when they returned home.

'What a pair you make.' Sky beamed as Evie returned to her larger size.

'What do you mean?' Cathy pressed as she tried to understand Sky's excitement.

'You were destined to be as one. That is why Evie was given to you. Look at your hand.'

Lowering her gaze, Cathy gasped as she saw the same pattern of lines and spot up her arm where she had touched Evie. At first she expected to feel pain but soon realised the glowing marks were somehow beneath her skin. Pressing her other hand to her arm, Cathy expected to feel heat, but there was nothing.

'How?'

'It seems you have both connected with your true potential, discovered your connections and in turn that has brought you closer together.' Sky moved Cathy's hand back to Evie's fur and smiled as the pattern glowed brighter on the two of them. 'Call the Eternal Flame.'

Cathy moved to retrieve the Aralcym, but Sky stopped her.

'Open your hand.'

Awash with curiosity, Cathy raised her open hand and watched as Sky took a tentative step back from her. Urging Galastial and Flash to keep their distance, he turned to Cathy and offered a simple nod.

'What do you want me to do?'

'Call the Flame in your hand.'

'I only just used it with the Aralcym. You can't expect me to say come here and it will respond, do you?'

As soon as the words left her lips, Cathy was astonished to see a ball of fire materialise in the air above her open palm. Wide-eyed, she stared at the dancing orb of fire as it grew to the size of a tennis ball between her fingers.

'Now shape it.' Sky encouraged, keeping his distance.

'Into what?'

'Whatever you want.'

Cathy stared at the orb of fire as she tried to find something to shape it into. With no conscious thought, the orb quivered in the air and took shape before her eyes. Staring at the mass of red, orange and yellow, she watched the ball turn into an all too familiar face, that of her mother.

'Beautiful.' Flash gasped.

'Wonderful.' Sky agreed as she moved to stand closer to Cathy. 'Of all the things you could have made, you made your mother's face.'

'Was that wrong?'

'Not at all Cathy. I'm sure Timothy would have fashioned a weapon of some sort and Aiden, well who knows what he would have made.'

'A games console controller, no doubt.' Cathy chortled.

'A what?'

'Doesn't matter.' Cathy stifled her laugh, not wanting to ruin the moment. 'I guess I made mum because I'm scared I won't see her again.'

'The Dark Queen's activation of the Gonks-Venit has opened this and many other portals between our worlds. As we speak, the gaps between our worlds grow smaller and we risk a convergence. If you are to see your family again, I fear you must once again stand in front of the Dark Queen.'

'I don't think making my mum's face is the same as fighting against her.' Cathy allowed the flaming face to evaporate from her palm.

'Our worlds need you to.' Sky replied. 'And with Evie by your side, you are no longer lost and disconnected from Mielikuvitus, the Eternal Flame or, more importantly, yourself.'

'I don't know.'

'I do.'

Sky's declaration was somehow reassuring to hear. Knowing that he believed in her to such an extent filled Cathy with pride. Taking a deep breath in, she turned to look at Evie, who offered her nothing more than a wink.

'Are you coming with me?'

'I can't, not yet. You must return to your family and join them as a Partum Spiritus.'

'But am I-' Sky silenced her with a raised hand and a stern look.

'That doubt is no longer welcome. You have grown in your family's image and stand now before us a guardian of our world, and your own. Self-belief has always been your greatest weakness, now let it become your strength.'

'Ok.'

'Then we should move, we haven't much time.'

Sky once again looked to the swirling portal above the arena and Cathy felt a sense of dread, knowing she would very soon be standing in front of the Dark Queen.

'I've got a question.'

'What's that?'

'Who is the Dark Queen's dad? She said her dad wasn't able to achieve his power and it was her birthright to rule both worlds. Was it the Dark Entity.'

A sudden seriousness washed over Sky as he stared up at the Gonks-Venit portal. After a long sigh, he turned to look at Cathy and dropped to his knees to meet her gaze.

'The Dark Queen,' Sky struggled to find the words. 'She is my daughter.'

Cathy's eyes grew wide as she looked at the troubled look on Sky's face.

CHAPTER TWENTY-FIVE

A FAMILY MATTER

Susan felt a sudden sting of pain as the Dark Queen swiped her weapons through the air. Having sensed the movement, she turned her head as the sand exploded where her head had been. Using her momentum to right herself, Susan re-ignited the Efiwym and turned to face her opponent.

'I want my daughter.' Susan snarled as Gerard moved to join her.

'We want our daughter.' He corrected and took his place by his wife's side.

Unwilling to discuss anything, the Dark Queen withdrew her swords from the ground and launched another attack. The ferocity and expertise of her attacks kept both Gerard and Susan on the back foot as they struggled to black and parry each strike. Grateful to be surrounded by the sea of fog that surrounded the small beachhead, they birthed even larger flames in an attempt to push the Dark Queen back.

'Dad!' Tim's voice carried in the air as Gerard dodged aside another expertly aimed thrust.

Casting a glance at his sons, his heart sank as he watched Aiden fly through the air as the Argyle smashed its armoured head into him.

'Get to the boys.' Susan growled through gritted as she wrapped the Eternal flame around her body.

Knowing his sons needed his help, Gerard offered her a smile and sprinted across the beach towards his boys. Left alone, Susan snaked the tendril of Eternal Flame around her body and waited for the next attack.

'You delay the inevitable.' The Dark Queen hissed as she watched Susan with an air of curiosity. 'You should accept your fate and step aside.'

'Not a chance.'

'So be it.'

The Dark Queen leapt forward but only made it two steps before she skidded to a halt. Having allowed the Eternal Flame to wrap around her torso, Susan called all her strength and concentration to bear as she enveloped her entire body in the living flame.

In an instant, Susan became a walking woman of fire. All of her features were displayed on the surface of the dancing flame and the Dark Queen gasped at Susan's skill and power of the fire.

'This is not possible.'

'You're clearly not a mother.' Susan bit as she dropped into an almost feline pose. 'A mother would do anything to protect her family and her children.'

With such a simple declaration, Susan launched herself through the air and took the fight to the Dark Queen. Suddenly on the back foot, the Dark Queen struggled to keep Susan at bay as she now fought without weapons, instead using herself as the weapon to protect her family.

Blow after blow, Susan ducked and dodged and found pleasure each time her fist or foot collided with the Dark Queen. Sensing another attack, the Dark Queen feigned a block but quickly corrected the course of her blades and swiped both up towards Susan's chest.

Susan had anticipated the attack and, at the same time as the strike, she launched herself up into the air and over the Dark Queen's head. Dragged by the momentum of her furious attack, the Dark Queen gasped as her blades did not meet their target and she felt a sudden solid blow in the small of her back.

Susan's surprise attack sent the Dark Queen crashing to the sand, dropping both her weapons as she fell.

Gerard arrived at the Argyle as it turned its attention to Timothy. Much to Gerard's pride, he saw Timothy create a sword and shield from his Nosym and held back the attacks of the armoured monster.

In all the times he had crossed to Mielikuvitus, Gerard had never seen anything like the Argyle. There was something almost devilish about the dark-skinned creature and how the metal armouring complimented the shimmering flesh. As he skidded across the sand beneath its stomach, Gerard raised his Nekorb and dragged the fire-blade across its underside.

Expecting to hear a shriek of pain, and the air to fill with the smell of smouldering flesh, his heart sank as the oily black flesh showed no signs of damage. The only sign the flame had collided with the Argyle was a line of smoke that wafted in the air.

'Tim, get Aiden.'

The moment Gerard spoke, the Argyle turned its attention to him. Swooping its enormous armoured head to look beneath its body, Gerard found his momentum stopped as the Argyle stamped its back foot into the sand. Colliding with the solid leg, Gerard felt the air rush from his lungs as his movement ended abruptly.

Rolling across the sand, Gerard rolled to both sides as the Argyle stamped its foot down on the ground in an attempt to squash him. Steering clear of the razor-sharp claws that gouged gulleys in the sand, Gerard kicked off from the Argyle's leg to get distance from the powerful stamps.

'Dad, look out!' Aiden screamed as the Argyle swept its spiked tail through the air.

Having no other choice, Gerard leapt into the air and wrapped his arms around the wide tail as it swept through the space he had been stood. Holding on for dear life, his Nekorb dropped to the sand. The Argyle sensed Gerard on its tail and thrashed around violently in an attempt to dislodge him.

Timothy saw an opportunity. Having not made it to Aiden, he changed his course and sprinted back towards the Argyle. The terrifying creature's attention was still fixed on his dad and it was too much of an opportunity to miss. Extinguishing the shield from his arm, Timothy scrambled underneath the Argyle and scooped up the bound handle of his father's weapon.

Armed with a weapon in each hand, Timothy trusted himself and took a moment to catch his breath as he emerged out behind the thrashing monster. Hearing his heart pounding in his chest, Timothy fought with the waves of fear and uncertainty to birth the flame in both his own Nosym and his father's Nekorb.

It was something he had never tried before. In reality, it had been many months since he had even tried to call the Eternal Flame to his command. Away from Mielikuvitus, the effort was so much more, and something Timothy feared was beyond him.

Ignoring the pounding in his ears and the niggling doubt in his mind, he recalled the feeling of control he had found when facing the Dark Entity in the Neverending Caves. Feeling the warmth in his skin, Timothy felt the Argyle's tail swoosh over his head but kept his eyes clamped shut.

'Now Timothy, now.'

Aleobe's voice was all he needed to hear as Timothy opened his eyes and teased the Eternal Flame from all four open mouths of the two weapons in his hands. Screaming with effort, Timothy created two double-edged swords and thrust them out towards the Argyle.

The flaming blades crashed into the whipping tail and while the flame did not breach the oily flesh, they did enough to stop the Argyle's tail from moving. Taking advantage of the distraction, Gerard released his grip and slid down to Timothy's side. Handing the Nekorb back to his dad, the two of them fought side-by-side as the Argyle rounded on them.

Aiden brushed himself down as the Argyle focussed on his younger brother and dad. Seeing his mother, now a womanly figure of flame moving with incredible speed, he suddenly felt surplus to requirement. Wondering what to do, Aiden was about to move when the spiked tail crashed into his side.

It was not an aimed attack, more a consequence of its positioning, but the scream of pain that echoed around the foggy bay brought everyone's attention to Aiden. With no chance to react, Aiden had been unaware of the Argyle's tail as it swept through the air. With the way he was standing, the first thing Aiden knew was as the first of two boned spikes crashed into his right shoulder and pierced the skin.

Feeling the rough bone tear into his shoulder, Aiden was filled with a burning pain that ripped through his body. Hoisted from the ground by the momentum of the powerful tail, he was once again thrown through the air as he slid off the two spikes.

'Aiden!' Susan shrieked as she turned to look at her oldest son.

Where he crashed into the sand, Aiden left a trail of stained sand in his wake until he smashed into an outcrop of rock on the side of the beach. Dazed and confused, Aiden rolled onto his side and came to rest, facing away from his family.

'All of you will fall.' The Dark Queen growled as she smashed the handle of one sword into the side of Susan's head.

As she staggered away, Susan lost her control over the Eternal Flame and, in a heartbeat, she was once again exposed in her human form, no longer covered by the dancing flames. Ignoring the pain in her head, Susan was no longer concerned by the Dark Queen as she ran to her son's side.

Dropping to the sand, Susan rolled him to face her and saw Aiden's face already bruised and swelling. Tracing her hands across his chest, Susan found the jagged wound in his shoulder and tried her best to make him comfortable. Leaning closer, she held her breath in the hope she would hear Aiden breathing.

To her relief, although ragged and laboured, she could hear her son breathing.

'Love is your greatest weakness.' The Dark Queen mocked as she slid the tip of her sword beneath Susan's chin. 'To be truly powerful is to be alone.'

In no position to resist, Susan allowed her head to be tilted up as she cradled Aiden in her arms. Turning her attention from her son, Susan looked up at the Queen whose sinister face was filled with childish glee. Allowing her a moment to survey her surroundings, the Dark Queen knew Susan was defeated.

Susan's attention moved from the Dark Queen to the Argyle that stood victorious with both Timothy and Gerard pinned beneath each of its front legs. Allowing her shoulders to sag, Susan knew her family had failed. Despite everything they had faced, everything they had overcome, it was in their own world that they would fall. Grateful to be hidden by the bank of swirling fog, Susan raised her teary gaze to the Dark Queen and took a deep breath in.

'I would have wished you to see the convergence of our worlds and the one I will create in its wake. ' The Dark Queen soothed with menace. 'But I have seen your family's strength and would not risk my success simply to revel and celebrate your defeat.'

'Do what you like.' Susan spat and closed her eyes.

The Dark Queen could not hold back her smile as she raised both her crackling words into the air. Preparing to attack, she took a moment to survey what she had achieved in besting not one, but four Partum Spiritus, something even the Dark Entity had never achieved. In that moment, she knew she was strong enough to fulfil her birthright and unite both worlds and shape them in her image.

With both weapons raised, she tightened her grip on the ornate handles and prepared to deliver the killing blow to Susan.

'Get away from my mum.'

The Dark Queen span around as Cathy emerged through the swirling portal. Riding on Evie's back, she landed on the sand as Evie unleashed a terrifying growl. Curling her lip in the Dark Queen's direction, Evie dropped low to allow Cathy to dismount from her back. Tendrils of blue smoke danced in the air between Evie and Cathy as she moved to stand by Evie's side.

'That's not possible.' The Dark Queen gasped as she saw the shimmering pattern on Cathy's arm that matched the pattern on Evie's fur. 'I killed you Hecate, I watched you die.'

'I said get away from my mum.' Taking a defensive position, Cathy unclipped her Aralcym and pointed it towards the Dark Queen. 'Now.'

CHAPTER TWENTY-SIX

BELIEVING

Cathy wasn't sure what had changed, but she felt stronger and more confident with Evie once again by her side. The fact her best friend was now almost ten times as big had something to do with it, but it was deeper than that. The moment she had touched the glowing pattern on Evie's fur, she had felt a connection much stronger than ever before. It was as if in that moment they became a single entity, connected and of a like mind.

With the same pattern of tiger stripes and leopard spots in pearlescent colours on her own arm, Cathy knew they were almost as one. As Evie's growl reverberated in the air of the fogged in beachhead, Cathy glared towards the Dark Queen with her swords raised above her mum's head.

'If you thought me dead,' Evie snarled, 'you are more foolish than I thought.'

'Who are you to speak to me?' The Dark Queen bit and turned to face the pair of new arrivals. 'How did you move past my armies?'

'They weren't that hard to beat.' Cathy replied with a wry smile as she saw the wave of concern dance on the Dark Queen's face. 'Probably better when they could see their beloved queen.'

Cathy's tone struck a nerve with the Dark Queen as she stalked across the sand towards her, leaving Susan alone with Aiden. Although Cathy had glimpsed her dad and Tim trapped by the Argyle, she knew she had to remain focussed on the Queen above all else.

'Cathy, please.' Aleobe's voice hushed in her ear. 'Tim needs your help.'

'Not now.' She hissed in reply as the Queen closed her down.

The attack came without warning, but Evie was quick to react. Having halved the distance between them, the Dark Queen leapt into the air and summoned a bolt of lightning from the turbulent sky above. Expecting what was coming, Evie absorbed the bolt of electricity as she flew above Cathy's head.

Ducking from the sudden crash of thunder, Cathy looked up to see Evie land on the sand and turn around in place. Every hair on her body rippled and crackled as the luminescent pattern glowed every brighter. Absorbing the sudden surge of electricity, Evie's eyes glowed white and Cathy could feel a tingle across her arm where the matching pattern traced across her own skin.

'Abomanation.' The Dark Queen shrieked as she leapt forward towards Evie.

Cathy acted on pure instinct. Gripping the Aralcym in her right hand, she fashioned a long spear out of the Eternal Flame and thrust it out towards the blue-haired Queen. Surprised by the sudden attack, Cathy smiled as the flaming tip of her weapon scratched across the breastplate of the Dark Queen's armour. Seeing sparks and flames erupt from the snake-embossed metal, the Queen was knocked aside by Cathy's attack.

Evie pounced in a heartbeat as the Queen reeled from Cathy's blow. She only just managed to cast aside the solid paw that hammered down on her with a flick of the weapons in her hands. The first missed its mark while the second scratched across the underside of Evie's paw, gouging a large cut across the largest leathery pad.

Cathy saw Evie rip her paw back at the sudden pain and timed herself for another attack. Fuelled by whatever magic connected her and Evie, she felt the sting of pain in her own hand but ignored its meaning. Not daring to give the Dark Queen any chance of retaliation, Cathy thrust and attacked as fast as she dared, all the while pushing the Queen back further across the beach.

As her spear hooked beneath the Queen's elbow, Cathy yanked it upwards and disarmed the sword she had held in her hand. The moment it left her hand, the surface of crackling electricity ended and all that landed on the sand was a lifeless handle.

Still armed with a single blade, the Dark Queen focussed her attention and did her best to counter the sudden furious attacks that Cathy rained in her direction. There was no denying that Cathy's connection with Evie had given her a renewed control over the Eternal Flame. Despite being on the defence, the Dark Queen scorned herself for being so quick to despatch the Hecate and wished she had kept the pair together and brought about the portals opening sooner than she had.

Distracted by her thoughts, Cathy seized the sudden lapse in concentration and dragged the full length of the spear's flaming blade down from the Queen's shoulder to her hip. The attack was delivered with such ferocity that the chest plate armour was cut neatly diagonally and fell into two pieces to the sand as it separated from her torso.

Knowing that Cathy was in the best position to push back the dark Queen, Evie took advantage of the fact the Dark Queen had forgotten about her and moved to aid Timothy and Gerard. Although the Argyle was easily twice the size of Evie, she still offered the oily-skinned armoured monster a challenge as she leapt through the air and sank her teeth into the back of the Argyle's neck.

The Argyle scream and raised onto its back legs, swiping to dislodge Evie from its back. The reaction had been what she wanted as both Timothy and Gerard were now free from the pressure of the Argyle's powerful legs. Half-buried in the soft beach sand, Gerard scrambled free and dragged his youngest son free before the Argyle's front legs smashed into the ground again.

Sprayed with a blast of sand, Gerard scooped Timothy behind him as Evie dropped from the Argyle's neck.

'I see you've had your moment.' Gerard quipped as he admired Evie's new appearance. 'How did Cathy take it?'

'She's done well.'

For a second Timothy looked up in surprise to hear Evie speak. Despite having spent his life sharing secrets with an invisible friend, hearing the family dog talk was something of a surprise. The fact Evie had grown in size was inconsequential to him, it just acted as a reminder at the strength of the magic from the world behind the mirror.

'Care to give me a hand with this beast?'

'My pleasure.' Evie barked and propelled herself under the Argyle and towards its spiked tail.

'Well, she's not wasting any time.' Gerard chuckled as he looked down at Timothy.

Taking Evie's lead, father and son launched into action and ignited the Eternal Flame from their sand-covered weapons. Working as a trio, they set about keeping the Argyle guessing as to where the next attack would come. Timothy led the charge and found a narrow gap at the side of the Argyle's head between the battered helmet and its mottled flesh. Feeding the blade of his Nosym into the gap, the Argyle once again shrieked in pain as a trickle of thick green blood seeped from beneath the armour.

'Keep going, we've got its attention.'

Not needing any more encouragement, Timothy set about scurrying beneath the enormous beast in search of other areas of weakness around the Argyle's helmet and head.

As the echoes of the Argyle's screams carried in the air, Cathy dared not move her attention from the Dark Queen. Despite having been disarmed of one of her weapons, it had done little to deter her from attacking. Although her armour had been cut from her body, the Queen now seemed to move with greater care, like a wounded hunter still intent on stalking its prey.

'You don't belong here.' Cathy's mum screamed as she launched an attack from behind.

Although Susan moved with astonishing speed, the Dark Queen easily cast aside the sudden attack. Driving her sword down behind her, the Queen dropped to her knees and succeeded in propelling Susan up and over to come crashing down by Cathy's side. Removed of the restrictive armour, she had a renewed speed and skill that caught Cathy by surprise.

'None of you belong in my new world.' The Queen spat as she rested the sword on her shoulder and pointed the tip towards Cathy.

'This isn't your world.'

'Not yet.'

What happened next filled Cathy with an unshakeable feeling of dread. With the crackling blade resting on her shoulder, the Dark Queen swept it around behind her head, dragging it through the air in a wide arc. As the trail of electricity arced behind the blade, Cathy saw something take shape behind the Queen.

Wide wings stretched either side of a slender figure whose eyes burned blood red. Seeing the eyes, Cathy felt a shiver down her spine. Timothy had spoken of the burning eyes in his nightmares when he was younger, but it had always been the Dark Entity. Seeing the eyes for herself, she understood why, when he had been her age, the sheer sight in his nightmares had terrified him.

'I am the one true force capable of calling the darkness to my will.'

'You're no different from the Dark Entity, or any of the others who sought power.' Susan replied as she moved to Cathy's side.

'How am I not different?' The Dark Queen lowered the sword to her side and allowed the manifestation of black smoke and electricity to take its position standing behind her. 'Were they not all vessels of darkness, nothing more than shells in which it could occupy and control?'

'Just like you.' Cathy spat.

'I control the darkness where they were controlled by it.' The Queen's wretched smile was filled with self-absorbed pride in her power. 'Bring them to me.'

Acting on her command, the figure of smoke and electricity stepped over her and launched towards mother and daughter. Slamming a crackling fist down towards them, Susan shoved Cathy hard and sent her crashing to the sand. Before Cathy could react, she was peppered with pieces of glass where the ferocious attack collided with the sand, super-heating it.

Grateful for the mask covering her face, Cathy heard the glass scratch across the mask's surface and felt the sting as the pieces scratched across her exposed arms. Shielding herself from the shards of hot glass, Cathy was about to move when the Dark Queen's beast slammed into her.

Once again, her muscles went taut as wave after wave of electricity coursed through her body. Dropping to the ground, she was powerless to fight back as the manifestation pinned her to the ground and pounded its free hand down on top of her.

Blow after blow, Cathy could do nothing to fight back. Staring up through the eyeholes of the mask, she focussed on the glowing red eyes that glared down at her. As the fist of electricity crashed down on her for a fifth time, the mask covering her face cracked. Hearing the material stress and buckle, Cathy feared the next blow would be the final one.

'Stop.'

Much to her surprise, it was not her mother's voice that froze the creature in position; it was the Dark

Queen's. With its hand raised above its head, ready to strike at any moment, Cathy was still pinned to the ground, with her muscles locked and unmoving.

'Let her go.'

Obediently, the creature released its grip on Cathy and she once again felt in control of her own body. Gasping for breath and fighting against the darkening edges of her vision, Cathy raised a shaky hand to her face. Sitting up, the lower third of her mask fell from her face, exposing her mouth and chin while the upper portion remained in place.

Shaking away the foggy haze, Cathy turned and felt her heart sink as the Dark Queen was now crouched by Aiden's side with the blade of her sword pressed into his neck. Still unconscious from the attack, Aiden was oblivious as to what was happening, but both Cathy and her mother knew what the Dark Queen was planning.

'Leave my boy alone.' Susan hissed through gritted teeth.

'Surrender yourself to me and I will spare your lives.'

Still distracted by the Argyle, Timothy, Gerard and Evie were oblivious to the turn of events on the beach's edge. Cathy took one look at her mother and knew they had reached the end.

CHAPTER TWENTY-SEVEN

STALEMATE

The Dark Queen pressed the blade into Aiden's neck but he showed now sign of knowing what was happening. His battered face looked swollen and while his eyelids flickered, they didn't open.

'I won't tell you again.'

As she spoke, the Argyle released a piercing scream as Evie had somehow managed to rip off the armoured helmet that covered its head. Now lying half-buried in the sand, Cathy watched as her dad lassoed a rope of fire around the giant creature's neck. Dropping to the beach, Gerard pulled tight and turned his attention to the Dark Queen and his oldest son.

'Let him go.' Gerard huffed as he fought to catch his breath. 'Or I'll kill this thing.'

Timothy wasted no time in helping his dad as he Argyle thrashed its head in an attempt to break free. For all his strength, Gerard could only hold the creature secure for so long as he found himself being dragged slowly back across the sand. Copying his dad's manifestation of the Eternal Flame, Timothy hooked his own weapon around the Argyle's neck and pulled in the opposite direction.

'It is but a beast to me.' The Dark Queen mocked as she ran her fingers through Aiden's hair. 'This boy, however, he is your blood and I know you would do anything for him.'

There was true menace in her word, and she shifted her gaze across each of the family in turn. At last, she settled her glare on Cathy who remained steadfast by her mother's side.

'You'll hurt him anyway.' Cathy replied as she tightened her hand on the Aralcym handle.

'You're probably right.'

They were at a stalemate, neither side wishing to give into the other and yet the Dark Queen knew she had the upper hand ultimately. A sudden movement in the fog stole everyone's attention as a silhouetted figure broke through the swirling mist and slowly came into view.

'Who's there?' Timothy hollered as the figure moved towards them.

At first it was difficult to see anything of the new arrival's features, all that could be seen was a small-statured figure moving with great care through the swirling fog. At last, as they moved through to the less dense area, Timothy gasped and released his grip on the Nosym in his hands.

Taking advantage of the distraction, the Argyle ripped its head upwards in an attempt to break free from the fiery restraints around its neck. The move was ill-advised as Gerard counteracted the sudden flex of its neck and in only swift movement severed the Argyle's head from its body.

As the enormous beast's body crashed to the ground, Timothy's attention did not shift from the new arrival.

'You?' Timothy stammered as he backed away from the shrouded figure.

The old woman from the house appeared in view but it was her aged face that stole Timothy's attention. Although it had been many years since he had last seen her, and somehow she was much older than she should have been, there was no denying the old woman was Dr Live.

'Hello Timothy.' Dr Live croaked as she shuffled across the sand.

'What are you doing here?' The Dark Queen snapped a she took in Dr Live's appearance.

'I didn't have a choice.' The old doctor replied as she lifted her bound hands.

Dr Live's hands were bound by a length of rope that dangled down between her legs. Although she walked alone, Timothy understood what was happening as he realised it had been Aleobe and Theo who had bound the old doctor and forced her onto the sand.

'Show yourselves you dirty little Ecilop.'

With a click of her fingers, the entire beach was bathed in a strange golden light. Spreading like a soundwave from her fingers, a ring of shimmering sparks travelled in concentric circles away from the Dark Queen until it touched the invisible flesh of the two hovering Ecilop behind Dr Live.

Aleobe offered Timothy a coy smile as he pressed a short dagger into Dr Live's back while Theo hovered just in front of the old woman as if guiding the way. Reaching the space between the motionless Argyle, Dark Queen and Cathy, the pair brought Dr Live to a stop.

Gerard moved in a heartbeat and rounded on the bound woman with ease. Bring his arm around her neck he made a point of bringing the handle of his Nodwons up into the same position as the Dark Queen's weapon on Aiden's throat.

'Check.' Gerard hissed as he teased a tendril of flame from the open maw closest to the doctor's neck. 'Somehow I don't think you'll disregard her as much as you did your little pet.'

'Seems we have a stalemate.'

'That we do.'

The section of sand between the Dark Queen and the family suddenly grew darker as a large circle appeared on the ground. Formed by some unseen magic, a solid portion of black rock rose from the ground. Looking down, Cathy recognised it to be the same stone that had bene used to construct the arena where she had been held prisoner.

'It seems the fairest way to settle this is with a fair contest.' The Dark Queen rose to her feet and wrapped a length of crackling electricity around Aiden's body.

Despite being unconscious, the sudden convulsion in Aiden's body was unmistakable and Susan moved to step forward.

'Let him go.' Susan hissed as she watched her son's body tense.

'We know that isn't gong to happen.' The Dark Queen smirked as she stepped onto the raised platform of jet-black rock. 'But you can end it.'

'How?'

'Let your daughter face me.' She offered an evil grin at Cathy. 'She's the reason for all of this after all.'

'You would fight a girl whose powers are nothing against yours?'

'Her powers equal yours.'

'But her skills do not.' Susan bit back. 'Face me.'

The Dark Queen considered Susan's offer for a moment before offering her nothing more than a dismissive nod, accepting Susan's challenge as if it was of no concern to her. Stalking across to the far side of the raised plinth, she locked gazes with Dr Live who said nothing.

'Mum, don't do it.' Cathy snatched at Susan's hand and pulled her back.

'I have to my love, we know what we are.'

'What you are, you mean? I'm the one who made this all happen.'

The regret and defeat in Cathy's tone was palpable in the air and it stopped Susan in her tracks. Glaring at the Dark Queen, she turned and faced her daughter. Despite all her ability to hide her emotions and hold her ground with her brothers, Cathy looked her age in that moment. The vulnerability in her eyes ignited a fire in Susan as she dropped to her knees and held Cathy's shoulders to speak with her.

'You are the same as me, you've just not learned to control it yet.'

'I don't feel like it. She's only here because of me.'

'She's here because of all of us, because we are the only thing stopping her from doing something we have fought for generations to hold back. This was always going to happen. If it wasn't her, it would be another fool who thinks the worlds are theirs.' Susan took a deep breath and placed a kiss on Cathy's forehead. 'But we are Partum Spiritus, in this world or theirs. We are sworn to protect, and that's exactly what I'm going to do.'

Filled with determination, Susan cast a loving glance at Gerard before stepping up onto the raise platform of darkened rock.

'Ready?' The Dark Queen sneered as she toyed with the remaining sword in her hand.

'Wait!' Cathy interrupted and threw her Aralcym to her mother.

Catching it, Susan offered her a smile and turned to face the Dark Queen.

'Now I am.'

That was all that was needed as the Dark Queen launched her first attack at Susan and the fight began.

Powerless to do anything but watch, the rest of the family looked on as the Dark Queen and Susan fought. The match was equal between the two of them. Their skills and control over the dark magic and Eternal Flame were matched, and neither held an advantage over the other. Despite being equipped with two weapons, Susan could not find advantage over the Dark Queen as she moved and dodged around most of her attacks.

More than once Susan felt the sting of the crackling blade across her arm and back, but not enough to disarm her or hinder her attacks. Biting back an outburst of frustration and the blade bit into her shoulder, Susan adjusted her position and thrust her Efiwym up through the air. Catching the Dark Queen by surprise, she manipulated the flame enough to hook it around her calf and rip her legs from underneath her.

Momentarily dazed by the sudden unbalancing, the Dark Queen blocked the follow-up attack and kicked out, forcing Susan to back away. Affording her enough time to move, the Dark Queen launched up from a crouched position and slammed into Susan, sending her falling from the battle platform.

The Dark Queen rained blow after blow down on Susan as they crashed into the soft sand. With her hands above her face, Susan dropped both her weapons and fought to take hold of the Queen's sword to keep her from using it against her.

Watching from the side lines, Cathy could see the desperation in her mother's face and saw the hilt of her Aralcym in the sand. Acting purely on instinct, Cathy ran to her mother's aid and scooped the handle from the ground. Knowing what was needed, fuelled by the desire to protect her mother and family, Cathy pointed the weapon at the Queen and screamed.

In response, a roaring fire exploded from both ends of the Aralcym and arced through the air to take the form of an enormous phoenix in the air. The sounds of rushing fire filled the air as the flaming feathered head turned to look at the Dark Queen.

'Leave her alone.'

As the words left her lips, the phoenix spread its wings and crashed down onto the Dark Queen, ripping her from on top of Susan. At first the Dark Queen fought back but as wave after wave of fire reigned down on her, the only sound that filled the air was Cathy's scream.

After what felt like an age, the screaming ended and Cathy collapsed to the floor, spent from the effort. Where the sand was scorched and glowing, shards of glass had formed from the immense heat, the Dark Queen lay unconscious and unmoving. What remained of clothes were now smouldering and flapping in the breeze while the her skin was scorched and dark.

Despite all that had happened, the Dark Queen was still breathing as she lay on the smouldering ground. Released from her dark magic, the surrounding fog evaporated, and the family once again found themselves bathed in the bright glow of the setting sun.

Moving to Cathy's side, Gerard disregarded Dr Live, and as the family ran to the aid of Cathy and Susan, the twisted doctor scurried away back to the eerie house on the cliffs.

'Cathy, are you alright?' Timothy asked as he dropped to her side.

'I'm fine.' Cathy coughed. 'What about mum?'

'I'm fine.' Susan answered as Gerard slipped his arm underneath her to help her up.

'Yeah I'm fine too.' Aiden spluttered as he sat up, no longer restrained by the Queen's bonds of electricity. 'Nobody cares about me.'

'Oh, shut up Aiden.' Cathy chuckled. 'I knew you'd be alright.'

A sudden sense of relief washed over the family as the sound of the lapping sea once again filled the air. Once Aiden had crawled to join them, Evie allowed herself to resume her familiar form and moved to sit by Cathy's side.

'I'm glad you 're ok.' Evie hushed as she pressed her cold nose to Cathy's cheeks.

'What are we going to do about that?' Cathy asked as she looked at the decapitated Argyle.

'I suppose I could help with that.' To everyone's amazement, it was Sky who answered as he stood on the sand behind them. 'We should move before your world wakes up again.'

Looking around, it was the first time Cathy realised that time had been frozen by the Dark Queen's crossing. The first thing she noticed was a Frisbee suspended in mid-air and the handful of seagulls in mid-flight.

As things started to move again, slowly at first, Sky ushered them back to Mielikuvitus. As had happened many times before, they all watched as the world around them faded and they passed through the void between the two worlds.

Chapter Twenty-Eight

The Fire Dome

Cathy was glad to be back in Mielikuvitus and even happier to see Painted Point stretching out in front of her as she opened her eyes.

'Welcome back.' Bubus-anjam declared as he lunged forward to hug Cathy tight. 'I had feared the worst when Sky brought Captain Flash back to me.'

'How is he?' Cathy quizzed, as she wrapped her hands around the aged cat's broad shoulders.

'He's seen better days but we've cleaned him up well.'

'I still smell like the sea though.' Flash boomed from behind them.

Cathy's smile lightened Flash's serious expression as he scanned around at Cathy and her family. Resting his weight on the cane in his hand, he beckoned Cathy to come to him and they shared a long hug.

'Thank you for saving me.' Cathy hushed as she placed a kiss on his furry cheek.

'You hardly needed my help.' Flash shrugged as he used his free hand to return the embrace. 'You're a warrior in your own right, puts this old sea captain to shame.'

'Hardly.' Cathy guffawed. 'You're still the best captain I know.'

'I'm the only captain you know.'

The pair shared a chuckle as they turned to face the surrounding crowd. To Cathy's relief, their return had been a small affair. Her family shared introductions with the faces gathered to welcome them back, and Cathy caught sight of her mother in deep conversation with Sky, away from the group. Even from a distance, she could tell their conversation was serious. Her mother's familiar furrowed brow told all she needed to know.

'This must be Timothy and Aiden?' Flash interrupted Cathy's silent curiosity and whispered in her ear. 'Leave them to discuss matters. I'm sure they'll talk to you about it sooner or later.'

Snatching herself back, Cathy knew Flash was right and shook off the concern about the hushed conversation between her mother and Sky.

'Yes, yes, this is Timothy and Aiden.'

'You've seen better days.' Flash remarked as he admired the rainbow of bruises across Aiden's face. 'You should see the old medicus, he has a way of helping this heal.'

'I'll admit I've got a bit of a headache.'

Aiden's face was swollen, bruised, and stained with dried blood. Although the electricity no longer coursed through his body, his muscles ached and he had secretly felt light-headed since they had arrived. Not wanting to make a scene, he had kept it to himself, but smiled at the offer of something to clear his head a little.

'With your permission, I would take him to see Galastial?'

'Of course.'

As Flash led Aiden away, Cathy realised her father had joined Sky, and both parents were now in deep conversation with the Elder. Alone with Timothy, there was an awkward silence between them. Aleobe had taken his usual position on Timothy's shoulder, yet they did not speak, instead Timothy's attention was focussed on the grand view in front of him. There was a hypnotic beauty about the city of reclaimed ships as it floated along the coastline. To Timothy, it looked like some curious painting you could find in a museum and he took a moment to drink in the curious beauty of his surroundings.

'You did good, little sis!' Timothy eventually hushed as he turned to look at his sister. 'I never thought it'd happen like this.'

'I only wanted to be as good as you.'

'It's not a competition.'

'That's rich coming from you.' Cathy chuckled. 'You're the sorest loser I know.'

Blushing, Timothy could not deny Cathy's remark. He had been known, on more than one occasion, to storm off from whatever game they had been playing, simply because he hadn't won. That said, they both knew that their destiny as Partum Spiritus was not a game.

'Doesn't change the fact I know how hard it is to find your way here.'

'I never thought I'd understand it or get it.' Cathy confessed as they both looked out across Painted Point. 'It seemed to take Sky forever to get me to do anything with my Aralcym.'

'He's an excellent teacher.'

'I know.'

'If it wasn't for him, I don't think any of us would be here. He even taught mum and dad to do it too.'

'How old is he?'

'I've never dared to ask. Seemed a little rude to ask him.'

'Do we have to go back home now?'

'I expect so.' They shared the same feeling of dismay, knowing their time in Mielikuvitus was inevitably ending. 'I always hated coming home.'

'I don't want to go home.'

'I know, I wish we could stay here forever.'

The pair fell silent as they looked at the activity on the far side of the floating town. The dockyard was a frenzy of activity as scores of creatures were busy constructing an all-too-familiar hull on the dry dock.

'They're making Flash a new ship.' Cathy declared as she pointed to partially constructed hull. 'They're making it look the same.'

'Do you know what I realise about Mielikuvitus?'

'What's that?'

'It's so much bigger than you think. I mean, I travelled to so many places when I was here and yet I never came here, until a few minutes ago I never even knew it existed.'

'Have you got any idea how big it is?'

'None at all. I wouldn't even dare to try and guess.'

'Cathy, Timothy, could you join us?' Sky's voice interrupted their train of thought.

Moving to join their parents and Sky, Aleobe whispered something in Timothy's ear that set a fresh flush to his cheeks. Fighting to hide the sudden embarrassment from whatever Aleobe had whispered, Cathy and Timothy waited for what was coming.

'Where's your brother?'

'Flash took him to see Galastial and get healed.'

'Good idea.' Sky nodded in agreement. 'Young Aiden has certainly seen better days.'

'Where's Evie?'

'She's going to meet us.'

'Where?'

'You'll see, soon enough.' Sky replied, continuing before Cathy could press with more questions. 'I've spoken with your parents and it would seem no matter how well we protect you, fate has something in store that keeps you connected to Mielikuvitus.'

'You mean we have to go back, don't you?' There was a sadness in Cathy's tone.

'We always have to go back.' Her mother answered. 'It is the only way to keep things moving. We are there to be called upon when needed. Otherwise we unbalance everything that keeps our worlds stable and separate.'

Cathy's shoulders dropped as she dropped her gaze to look at the wood beneath her feet.

'Oh, how you remind me of each other.' Gerard sighed as he rolled his eyes. 'The pair of you should have been twins.'

'Your father's right.' Sky agreed. 'Training you aboard the Lady Chance, Cathy, reminded me so much of Timothy's journey. And yes, your mother is right, you have to return home.'

'I suppose it's pointless to say we don't want to.'

'For all the reasons your mother just explained, yes.' Sky nodded in agreement. 'But going back this time will not be the same.'

'You mean we can keep visiting?' Cathy interrupted, a childish smile appearing on her face.

'Let Sky finish.'

'Sorry.'

'It would be nice to restore the balance between our worlds, but I fear the Dark Queen's actions may have altered that beyond repair.'

Sky lifted a large bound sack from the ground at his feet and reached inside. Awash with curiosity, both Cathy and Timothy craned to see into the sack as Sky withdrew his hand. In his hand, Sky held a gem the size of a grapefruit that glimmered in the sun. The gem was a fluorescent pink colour and the sun's rays reflected a pattern of shimmering pink on all of their faces.

'Is that?' Cathy gasped.

'One of the Gonks-Venit? Yes.' Sky handed Cathy the oversized gem.

The weight of the gem surprised Cathy. It felt no heavier than a feather as she admired the shimmering crystal, yet it felt sturdy and strong. Turning it over in her hand, she looked at the angular faces of the stone and realised a small flame danced in the heart of the translucent surface.

'What's it made of?'

'What is it?' Timothy added as she looked at the Gonks-Venit with curiosity.

'I'm sure your sister will explain.' Sky smirked, casting Gerard and Susan a knowing look. 'For now, we have removed them from the Dark Queen's control and closed the temporary portal created at the arena.'

'But?' Cathy pressed, knowing there was more, despite Sky's silence.

'When the worlds were temporarily aligned, the Dark Queen did not know that the portal at the arena was not the only one. Having spoken with Nasser, it would appear other parts of our worlds were temporarily aligned and we are yet to locate and close them.'

'I thought we had stopped the worlds converging.' Cathy looked away from the stone in her hand. 'You mean we didn't stop anything?'

'You stopped the convergence as it was at that time.' Sky sighed. 'A consequence of the Queen's actions was to create tendrils of connectivity between our worlds. While singularly none would be enough to draw the worlds together, their existence as a collective could do just that.'

'How many are there?'

'We are still finding out, but Nasser has already learned of three.'

'How many would it need to keep the worlds pulling together?'

'Nobody knows.' Sky replied, his words laced with concern. 'Think of the convergence as a spider. Its body was the point through which the Dark Queen travelled, and yet it has smaller legs to anchor it in place. Each leg still connects, but is not quite enough to make an impression or lasting mark.'

'So, what does that mean for us?'

'We shall return the Gonks-Venit to the Chigem Mines and the protection of the Chigems.' Sky removed the pink stone from Cathy's hands. 'But you and your family, when Aiden is rested, will return home to locate the remaining portals and close them.'

'These other portals,' Timothy quizzed, 'are they big enough for other things to come through or are they just spaces that need to be closed off?'

'That, my dear Timothy, we do not know. There is a possibility that creatures may have crossed, in either direction, but until we find them, we cannot be sure.'

'And if we don't close them off, what's this convergence thing?'

'Both worlds will cease to exist in independence and combine to create a new world. Life as we know it, for both sides of the portal, will end and something new will emerge in their place.'

'That's what the Dark Queen was trying to do.' Cathy continued, as she turned to look at her brother. 'She wanted to create a new world in her image and rule over it all.'

'Sounds wonderful!'

'What's happened to her anyway, the Dark Queen?'

There was a moment of awkward silence as her parents looked at one another. Sensing the unease, it was Sky who gave them the answer.

'Your parents think it best to keep that from you. I would seek to have you see.'

'See?'

'The Dark Queen lives. She is now a prisoner in our charge.'

'You mean, I didn't kill her?'

'Did you want to?'

The question caught Cathy by surprise, and she struggled to find the right answer.

'Death is not something you should concern yourself with. The protection of our worlds is first and foremost. The Dark Queen is, as was the Dark Entity and those before them, agents of evil. That fact does not make their life worth any less than ours.' Sky's words felt like a stern lesson for all gathered around him. 'We will be charged with her imprisonment, while you will be charged with limiting the damage caused by her dark desires to combine our worlds.'

'I think I understand.'

A sudden movement in her peripheral vision stole her attention as Evie wandered along the winding path towards them.

'Is it done?' Sky asked as Evie approached.

'The Fire Dome has been created and holds its place. The Dark Queen is secure.'

'Excellent.' Sky turned his attention to Cathy. 'Would you care to see?'

Answering with a nod, Sky ignored the glares from Gerard and Susan as he placed his arm around Cathy's shoulder and set off behind Evie.

'Guess that's settled that then.' Gerard sighed as he took hold of Susan's hand and they followed behind, with Timothy by their side.

CHAPTER TWENTY-NINE

FIT FOR A QUEEN

A dome of swirling fire sat over an isolated island off the shores of the Forgottenlands. In the distance, Cathy could make out the silhouette of the abandoned arena and felt a wave of dread wash over her. Casting aside memories of her battles on the sand, she turned her attention to the swirling dome and realised it was where Sky was guiding them.

Reaching the shoreline, it dawned on Cathy how big the dome was. As Sky moved his hands in the air, the fire became ever more see through until they could all see everything encased beneath the flaming prison.

The island was an unwelcoming affair. Jagged rocks and a handful of trees collected together, surrounded by a series of smaller portions of land. It was big enough to build a small settlement on, but nothing more.

'This is the Fire Dome.' Sky declared with pride. 'It will be the Dark Queen's home from now on.'

'Fit for a Queen, wouldn't you say?'

The Dark Queen's voice sounded unfamiliar, scratching and struggled whereas she had always portrayed herself with regal prowess. Cathy scanned around for the source of the voice but saw nothing, despite sounding as if the Queen was standing just on the other side of the now transparent walls of the dome.

'You would do well to remember the fortune in the fact you have life in which to spend in solitude.' Sky warned, the growl of his animal nature showing through in his words.

'Only because she could not do what was necessary.'

The Dark Queen appeared out of nowhere, hovering above the calm waters of the sea that separated the island from the shore. She no longer looked regal and royal. Every inch of that life had been eaten away by the flaming phoenix and now she hovered above the water dressed in tattered robes, her striking blue hair unkempt atop her head.

'I never wanted to kill you.'

'Hush Cathy, don't give her the pleasure of arguing.' Susan grabbed her daughter's hand and held it tight.

Looking up at her mother, she knew she was right and fell silent. Turning her attention back to the Dark Queen, Cathy felt a pang of sadness for her. Cathy remembered her as a powerful woman, dressed in her immaculate armour and lavish clothes and now she looked dishevelled, a shadow of her former self.

'I pity the fact you think this place will contain me.' The Dark Queen seethed with anger. 'You must know my armies will search for me and rip me from your imprisonment.'

'They will try.' Sky answered with barely a glimmer of emotion. 'We will hold them back, much as we have done with you.'

'You cannot alter the course of fate.' The Dark Queen slammed her hands against the walls and recoiled as her arms were engulfed in flame. 'I will arise a Queen above the lands of a combined world, shaped in my image.'

'Perhaps.' Sky shrugged. 'But while you reflect on your failures, we will seek to undo the mess you have created and dispose of the Gonks-Venit so they cannot be called forth to yours, or anyone else's, will again.'

'You cannot stop me.' The Dark Queen hollered.

'Of all the people across both worlds, we both know I can.' Sky took a deep breath as he turned his back on the Fire Dome. 'A father knows his daughter best, after all.'

'You are not my father.'

'Come, let's go.' Sky offered.

'That's what you've always done. Nothing changes. You always found it easy to turn your back on me and leave.'

As the Dark Queen continued to rain abuse towards the group, most being aimed at her father, they walked away in silence. Only when the Dark Queen's voice was no longer chasing them did Sky bring them to a stop.

'Your daughter?' Gerard asked, the accusation clear in his voice.

'A story for another time my friend.'

Gerard knew now was not the time to push and let the matter lie.

'What now?' Timothy finally asked in an attempt to break the awkward silence that had descended.

'We will see how Galastial has fared in healing Aiden and then I should see you on your path to closing the remaining portals.

As the group walked back through the heart of Painted Point, the Dark Queen was once again lost behind the swirling walls of fire that encased her and held her prisoner. Surrounded by the Forgottenlands, Bubus-anjam had navigated Painted Point to a position to hold guard over the Dark Queen.

So much had changed since Cathy had arrived in Mielikuvitus and somehow, as she walked with her friends and family, she felt different. When she had arrived, she had felt an underdog, overshadowed by the achievements and abilities of her family. Looking back, she now realised she stood equal to them, worthy to hold the Aralcym by her side.

Unconsciously her fingers traced along the length of the bound handle as the Aralcym hung by her side. Whatever Sky needed them to do, she knew they would succeed as a family. Casting one last glance back towards the Forgottenlands she saw the silhouette of the Dark Queen through the roaring fires.

It was time to go home.

It was time to protect everything, and everyone, she had come to love.

CATHY SCOTT WILL RETURN

Cathy's adventure will continue in **Cathy Scott: Venit Rings**, sign up to stay up-to-date at **www.tobey-alexander.com**.

Reviews

ENJOY THIS BOOK? YOU CAN MAKE A HUGE DIFFERENCE...

Reviews are the most powerful tool in helping me build trust in my stories and creativity. When it comes to getting attention for my books, there is nothing better than an honest word from someone who has entered my world and enjoyed the story I have told.

At the moment I don't have the power behind me to advertise on billboards or in newspapers (trust me, I'm working on it) but I do have something the big advertising agencies don't have and that's YOU!

An honest review shared, no matter how short, catches the attention of other readers and help give my books validity.

If you have enjoyed this book I would be more grateful than you can imagine if you would spend just a few moments leaving a review on the book's Amazon Page.

Thank you so very much for your time and I look forward to inviting you back for another adventure soon.

Printed in Great Britain
by Amazon

18503912R00140